MUFFLED SCREAM I
CORNER OF THE EYE

MUFFLED SCREAM I: CORNER OF THE EYE
EDITED BY DOUGLAS OWEN

WICKED TALES

http://wickedtales.ca
An imprint of DAOwen Publications
Copyright © 2016
Copyright of individual stories is retained by the authors

Muffled Scream I: Corner of the Eye
Edited by Douglas Owen
ISBN 978-1-928094-13-5
EISBN 978-1-928094-14-2

Jacket art: MMT Productions

10 9 8 7 6 5 4 3 2 1

Welcome to the first Muffled Scream, Wicked Tale's flagship theme based anthology focusing on the talents of Horror storytellers.

This anthology is a dream of our editor, who has been a lover of the written word since he first learnt to read. And since then he's searched for stories that challenge the mundane existence of this world.

After reading this collection of stories, please take the time to either rate or review it on GoodReads. This collection can only continue with your support and continued patronage.

For information on upcoming releases of the Muffled Scream anthology, visit our website, WickedTales.ca, or visit our Facebook.

More exciting books are available at:

https://daowenpublications.ca

Subscribe to our newsletter for exciting news and upcoming publications

Six Miles to Bastogne
Ambrose Stolliker

"Off your ass, Galloway. Lieutenant wants you inside."

Corporal Tom Galloway frowned at the sound of Sergeant Rawls barking orders at him and tried to hide the displeasure of having the first moments of silence he'd enjoyed in three days interrupted. He shouldered his rifle and followed Rawls through a stone gate leading up to a French country style farmhouse with a thatched roof. Next to the house were the smoking remains of a barn and windmill Galloway guessed had been leveled by German 88s. A four-inch layer of pristine white snow covered everything, lending an incongruous sense of beauty to the charred skeletons of the two buildings.

Inside, Galloway found Lieutenant Cargill warming his hands at a fireplace. Glad to be out of the cold, he decided giving up a few moments of silence might not be so bad after all, especially with the rest of the guys freezing their asses off outside. The house's owner, an old farmer dressed in a thick wool sweater and homespun pants, sat in a chair next to the hearth. On the mantle over the fireplace hung a sword and regimental colors. Galloway recognized them immediately. Rawls stood off to the side.

Galloway saluted Cargill. "Sergeant Rawls said you wanted to see me, sir."

"You speak French, right, Galloway?"

"And German, sir."

"Ask this frog how far we are from Bastogne."

Galloway turned to the farmer. A thin sheen of sweat had formed on the old man's forehead "Dans quelle mesure à Bastogne, s'il vous plait, monsieur?"

"Dix-sept kilometres. Si vous prenez la route."

"If we stick to the road, it's seventeen klicks. That's about–"

"Eleven miles, yes, I know the metric system, Galloway. Thank you." He turned to Rawls. "Is that truck fixed yet?"

Rawls shook his head. "No, sir. Doesn't look fixable. Private Cole says we'll be hoofing it back to the lines."

"How the hell does a perfectly functioning vehicle just stop working all of a sudden, Sergeant?"

Rawls shrugged. "Beats hell outta me, Lieutenant. It checked out before it left the lines this morning. Cole's had his head under the hood for the last three hours and can't find anything wrong with it."

"Well, it's damn peculiar, you ask me."

"Radio's onna fritz too, so we can't even call back for another truck."

"Wonderful." Cargill turned back to Galloway. "Ask him if there's a faster way back to Bastogne. Maybe through the forest?"

Galloway nodded and translated.

The farmer's eyes gaped. He started to get out of his chair. "Non! Non! Ne pas aller dans la forêt!"

"He says not to go through the forest." Without being prompted by the Lieutenant, Galloway asked, frowning, "Pourquoi?"

The farmer went quiet and sat back down, his eyes on the fire.

"Monsieur? Pourquoi?"

"Stay on the road," the old man said in French. "It's safer."

Galloway sighed. "Uh, he just says to stay on the road, that we'll be safer there."

Rawls reached between Galloway and Cargill and poked the farmer in the chest. "Don't give us any bullshit, buddy. We go in there and my guys get shot up by the Krauts I'm gonna come back here and pay you a visit, you hear me?"

Galloway maneuvered between Rawls and the farmer. "Lay off, Sergeant. The Germans've already destroyed most of what this man owns. Or didn't you notice?"

"Don't get smart, Corporal. And maybe if guys like him had fought a little harder when the Panzers rolled over France he'd still have a farm."

Galloway gave Rawls a smug grin, and nodded at the sword and regimental flag over the hearth. "He did fight. At the First Battle of the Marne."

"The Germans aren't anywhere near the Marne–"

"In 1914."

Rawls was momentarily flummoxed. Then, his brow furrowed and smoky fury simmered in his eyes. "You think you're so fucking smart, don't you, you little fu–"

"That's quite enough, sergeant," Cargill cut in. "You too, corporal."

"Sure, Lieutenant," Galloway said.

"Galloway, I have six German prisoners I need to get to Bastogne in the next twelve hours, one of whom is a high-ranking officer in the Sixth SS Panzer Army," Cargill said. "Every second he's not spilling his guts to Army Intelligence, American boys are dying needlessly. Now you ask this man whether there are any Kraut units in the forest between here and Bastogne, and tell him he better tell us the truth."

Galloway turned to the old farmer. "Monsieur," he said gently. "Are there any German soldiers in the forest?" He touched the man on the shoulder and gave him a soft smile. "Ne t'inquiete pas. Je ne laisserai pas cet animal te blesser." He nodded at Rawls as he spoke the last part of the sentence.

The old man smiled back at Galloway and his eyes brightened. "No. No Germans in the forest." Then, as quickly as it had appeared, his smile vanished. At the same time, the light in his eyes was replaced with an emotion with which Galloway had become intimately, painfully familiar since his unit had landed at Omaha Beach the month before. Fear. Galloway started to turn away when the old man spoke again for a few moments before looking back to the fire. Galloway wasn't sure how to respond to what the old man had just told him.

"Well, Corporal?" Cargill asked.

Galloway shook his head. "He's not making much sense, sir. He says there aren't any Jerry's in there, that some went in before the big battle, but they never came out." He faced the Lieutenant. "He says the forest is evil and we shouldn't go in there."

"Oh, for Christ's sake," Cargill groaned. "I don't have time for this back country superstition." He turned to Rawls. "Get the men up. We're moving out."

"Which way, sir?" Rawls asked.

"Get your map out, Galloway," Cargill said.

Galloway took out a topographic map of the Ardennes region and unrolled it. The lieutenant studied it for a moment and then pointed at a small patch of forest.

"We can bisect the forest and the road here," he said. "That'll put us where we need to be by early tomorrow morning at the latest." He rolled it up and handed it back to Galloway. "Six miles to Bastogne. As the crow flies."

As the crow flies. Great. Too bad we're not crows. "Sir," Galloway began, "maybe we should listen to this guy. He seems to know the area and – "

"I didn't ask your opinion, Corporal. You're dismissed. You too, Sergeant."

Galloway bit his tongue and ignored the self-satisfied grin on Rawls' face. He saluted Cargill and left the house, trying hard to put the look of fear in the old man's eyes out of his mind. The lieutenant was making a mistake here, he was sure of it, and all so they could get the SS officer to Army Intelligence where, like every other SS officer who had ever been captured, he would tell his interrogators exactly nothing. But that didn't matter to Cargill. He was the worst kind of officer – the kind who cared less for the welfare of his men than he did for the accolades of his superiors, accolades that would get him bumped up to captain. Galloway shook his head.

"What was it you said in there to that guy?" Rawls said, grabbing Galloway by the arm and interrupting his thoughts for the second time that day.

"I told him everything was going to be all right and I wouldn't let an animal like you hurt him." Galloway replied. "Was there anything else, Sergeant?"

Rawls let him go, but leaned in close so the other men, who had taken notice of their tense exchange on the farmhouse porch, wouldn't hear. "Better not turn your back on me in the forest, boy. You might not come out. Just like those Krauts."

"I'd like to see you try it, Rawls." He turned on his heel and left the farmhouse.

Galloway walked up to Jimmy Cole and slapped him on the shoulder.

Cole, who was all of five-six, hailed from Brooklyn and went through basic training with Galloway. "The hell was all that about?" he asked, nodding at the spot where he and Rawls had their face-off.

He leaned in close to Cole and quickly filled him in on what had transpired in the farmhouse – his confrontation with Rawls, the old man's strange warning and Cargill's decision to ignore it.

"So this farmer thinks the forest is haunted?" Coles' eyes narrowed with skepticism. "Get outta here." He looked at Galloway askance. "You don't believe that bullshit do you?"

He shook his head. "No. But it doesn't make a whole lot of sense to me to abandon a perfectly good road for a stretch of forest that just swallowed up a bunch of Germans."

"It's that SS officer, isn't it? That why Cargill wants to get back so fast." Then, he added under his breath, "Stupid son of a bitch."

Out of the corner of his eyes, Galloway saw Rawls glaring at them. "Come on. Let's get the prisoners down before Rawls finds some other reason to chew us out."

"Like he needs a reason."

They went to the back of the truck, a flatbed with a dark green canvas top, where Galloway nodded at two other men standing guard over the prisoners. The two men – Corporal Paul Blatty of Chicago and Private Ray Adelson of Oxnut, Mississippi – snapped back salutes and waited for orders from Galloway. There were four prisoners in all – three they picked up after abandoning their 88 millimeter cannon and an SS rittmeister, or captain. The three artillerymen were all enlisted and none looked over the age of twenty. The SS captain, however, had deep wrinkles and ridges on his face and a thinning head of gray hair. As a whole, their uniforms were dirty and worn with holes where there shouldn't be any. Only the SS captain had much in the way of winter gear. At first glance, he looked like most mid-rank field officers, but upon closer examination Galloway spotted the tell-tale SS insignia at the collar – the double lightning bolt "scharfuhrer" and the skull and cross bones "totenkopf" they'd all been taught to recognize in basic training.

"You men get down out of there," Galloway said to the prisoners in German. "We're leaving." When they didn't move, he barked, "Schnelle! Schnelle! Come on, let's go!"

The three boys looked to the SS captain, who nodded curtly at them, then slowly got up. All four were bound with their hands behind their backs. The SS captain was the first to jump from the lip of the flatbed. His steel grey eyes met Galloway's briefly and then he looked straight ahead without a word, moving only to make room for the three artillerymen.

Pretty cool customers, these SS boys. Better keep my eye on this one. "Over there," Galloway said, pointing to where the lieutenant and Rawls stood. Then, to Cole and the other two men, "Let's go. Fall in. We're heading out."

"Where we goin'?" Blatty asked. "They're sendin' another truck for us, right, Galloway?"

"We're hoofin' it, Blatty."

"Well, least we can't get lost on the road. It takes us straight back to Bastogne."

"We're not taking the road."

"Why the fuck not?" Blatty whined.

"Ask the lieutenant."

"I'm askin' you, Galloway."

"The lieutenant knows a short cut."

"Oh. Fuckin' great. Through where?"

"The forest."

"I'm not goin' through there!"

"Tell it to Rawls, Blatty. I really don't give a damn what you do." The truth was, Galloway hated Blatty, whom he had once counted as a friend. He was lazy and a kiss-ass and, worst of all, an informer. Galloway would be the first to admit to occasionally bending the rules, but he only did so out of concern for his friends. Twice while performing maneuvers in England, in preparation for the invasion of Normandy, Blatty had ratted on Galloway for stealing whiskey from the English officers' mess. All Galloway had wanted to do was give his buddies a break from the mounting pressure of what they were about to undertake. Though the charges were never proven and he was never caught red-handed, the incidents cost Galloway an extra set of stripes, a set of stripes that Blatty had hoped would end up on his sleeve. He'd been wrong. The stripes had gone to Rawls. Trying to make the best of a scheme that had backfired on him, Blatty had decided to throw his lot in with their new sergeant, who seemed to revel in having Blatty as a lapdog.

"Why can't they send another truck? We're supposed to be the goddam mechanized infantry, remember?"

"Because the radio in the truck's dead. We can't call. So, we're on our own."

Blatty gave him a dirty look and trotted past, leaving Galloway, Cole and Adelson behind. Adelson was the youngest member of their squad. He'd just celebrated his nineteenth birthday three days before the day the German siege of Bastogne had ended. A light-haired boy with blue eyes and a pale face, he walked up alongside Galloway and started to say something, then appeared to think the better of it. This went on for several minutes before Galloway stopped and turned to face him.

"Jesus, what is it, Adelson? If you want to ask me something then just ask me, all right?"

"Yes, sir–"

"You don't have to call me sir."

"Yes, sir."

Galloway rolled his eyes. "What was it you wanted?"

"Well, sir, I was just wonderin' if you might help me write a letter to my girl when we get back tomorrow."

Not long after joining the unit, Galloway had learned Adelson was the squad's whipping boy. He wasn't bright and his nasal, backwoods Mississippi accent made him an easy target for ridicule. Rawls and Blatty especially loved to pick on him. Within weeks of meeting Galloway, Adelson had glommed on to him like an adoring kid brother. Galloway pushed those thoughts aside and smiled at Adelson.

"A letter, huh? Who're you writing to this week, Romeo?"

"Uh, Betty, sir. Same gal as last week."

"I was kidding, Adelson."

"So, you'll help me?"

"No sweat."

"Thank you, sir. I ever show you a picture of my Betty?"

"Uh, yeah, about fifty times since–"

"Hey!"

Galloway turned. Rawls was barking at them again.

"Let's go, Galloway! Get those men up here on the double!"

"Yes, sir, Sergeant, sir!" Galloway yelled with mock enthusiasm. He gave Rawls a sharp salute, grinned at him like a perfect idiot and marched the four prisoners to Cargill, the sergeant and Blatty.

"Sergeant Rawls and I scouted ahead a little and found a patch of forest that might work for us," Cargill was explaining. "The way east is relatively clear and shouldn't give us too much trouble."

"Excuse me, sir?" Galloway put in.

"Yes, corporal, what is it?"

"What do you mean by 'relatively clear'? This is one of the densest parts of the Ardennes region."

For the briefest flash of a moment, Cargill looked uneasy, but he quickly covered it up. "Well, since you asked, Corporal, it looks like it's the same way the Germans the old farmer told us about went."

"You mean the Germans who never came out of the forest?"

Cargill gave him a poisonous look. "Yes, that's right, corporal. Any other questions? Good." He pointed past the still-dead truck down the road. "It's right around the bend there. Grab whatever gear from the truck you think you'll need, boys. We're moving out."

A few minutes later, Cargill, Rawls and Blatty were headed down the road. Galloway, Cole and Adelson brought up the rear, walking close behind the four Germans. Just as he was about to round the bend, Galloway turned and looked back at the farmhouse. The old man stood in the window, the orange glow of the fire dim in the background. His eyes were fixed on Galloway, who, after a moment, waved at him and gave him his best "don't worry about us, we'll be OK" smile. The old man closed his eyes, made the sign of the cross and disappeared from the window. A chill went through Galloway, and, for a moment, he forgot he was supposed to be escorting the prisoners into the forest. Something about the look in the old man's eyes just before he'd left the window really spooked him. It wasn't just fear he'd seen in them. There'd been something else. Sorrow. Pity even. Pity for him and his friends.

"Hey! Galloway! Get a goddam move on!"

Rawls again.

Galloway shook his head. *It's a wonder the whole German army doesn't know we're here with his big mouth. That guy's going to plant us all before this war is over, I swear.*

"C'mon, Tom!" Cole called after him, though it came out more like a hiss through his teeth so Rawls and Cargill wouldn't hear.

He jogged back into formation and soon they met up with the rest of the group. They stood at the edge of the road with their necks craned skyward to the tops of a massive cluster of towering pine trees. Having grown up in New England, Galloway was no stranger to forests, but he had never seen trees so monstrous in height. They reminded him of photos of the gigantic fir and hemlock trees in the Pacific Northwest that he'd seen in his father's issues of *Life Magazine*. There was something different about the trees though. Maybe it was a trick of the failing light, but their trunks were darker than he'd have expected them to be – black almost. Their bark was knotted and covered with bulbous growths that made the trees look pockmarked with disease. Their roots protruded gnarled and wet through a thick layer of dead leaves and snow like the tentacles of a creature from deep under the sea. The trees in *Life Magazine* had seemed majestic. Magnificent even. But these? Galloway found them grotesque. The looks on the other mens' faces revealed they pretty much thought the same thing, all except Cargill and Rawls, who seemed oblivious.

"Looks like the Krauts did a pretty nice job cutting through the thicker vegetation," Rawls said. Then, turning to the SS captain, he added snidely, "See? You guys can do something right. Besides gassing defenseless Jews."

Galloway rolled his eyes. On too many occasions to count, he'd heard Rawls say he didn't give a shit what the Nazis were doing to the Jews – "the kikes" – he called them. As far as Rawls was concerned, they were "pushy and money-grubbing" and had "gotten what was coming to them."

When the SS captain didn't acknowledge him, Rawls gave his shoulder a shove. "Yeah, you didn't think we knew about what you been doin' to the *Juden*, didja? Well, we do. Know what they're gonna do with all you SS boys when this thing is over? Line ya up and…" He aimed his weapon at the prisoners and made a machine gun sound with his tongue. The three artillerymen all jumped, but the SS captain didn't move, or even bother to make eye contact with Rawls. His stare remained on the forest directly ahead. This infuriated the sergeant.

"Or, better yet," Rawls continued, his mouth forming a sardonic grin, "maybe we do to you boys what you did to eighty of our guys at Malmedy. There're only four of you, but what the hell, it's a good start."

The brass had tried hard to keep a lid on it, but word had trickled down through the officers' ranks, and then the enlisted, of a massacre near Malmedy the month before. About eighty American prisoners of war had been machine gunned in a field by men from the 1st SS Panzer Division without warning or explanation. As if they needed any more reason to hate the Germans, the stories had left many American soldiers in the Ardennes region in a bloodthirsty and vengeful mood.

Refusing to be ignored, Rawls grabbed the SS captain's chin and forced the German to meet him eye to eye. "You hear what I'm sayin' to you, kraut? You're gonna be *dog meat* when Intelligence gets through with you – "

Cargill finally cut in. "That's enough, Sergeant. We need to get a move on. Release that man." When Rawls didn't move, the lieutenant raised his voice. "That's an *order*, Sergeant."

The SS captain's gray eyes remained impassive. If he was upset at being manhandled by Rawls, he didn't show any sign of it. Rawls let the man's chin go with a sullen flick of his fingers.

Galloway let out a sigh of relief. *Jesus. I thought the crazy bastard might shoot him right there.* He exchanged a look of unease with Jimmy Cole and knew his friend had been thinking the exact same thing.

"Let's go, people," Cargill said at the top of his lungs. "I want three miles of forest between us and this road by nightfall!" He turned to Galloway. "Give me your compass, Corporal and then get back there with the prisoners. I'll lead us out."

Galloway did as he was told, unslung the rifle from his shoulder and waited for the others to start their march. Then, shaking his head, he entered the forest as the moon rose and dusk settled across the land.

Just after nightfall, it was clear to Galloway the squad was lost. Their initial bearing was a wide, unnamed stream that bisected their route through the forest. The stream's location was directly due north and impossible to miss, yet somehow, they had. When Galloway broached the possibility they might be off course, Cargill turned on him.

"I know how to read a compass, corporal," he informed him. "And this one says we're headed north."

An hour later, Cargill called a halt to the march and stood at the head of the squad, hands akimbo. His head swiveled right, then left, as if one patch of forest might offer a clearer route to than the other. Finally, without turning around, he called to Galloway.

"Yes, sir?"

"Take this," he said, all but slapping the compass into Galloway's hand. There was acid in his voice. "It's broken. Get me one that works."

Galloway signaled Jimmy to hand over his compass. A moment later, the lieutenant continued in the same direction they'd been heading all evening, the compass held out in front of him. He'd gone no more than a few paces when he started shaking his head.

"Same damn thing. Sergeant Rawls, your compass."

Rawls handed it over. Cargill retraced his steps, then returned the instrument back to its owner.

"How is it possible that not one, but three compasses are out of whack? How is that possible?"

"Mine worked fine this morning, sir," Galloway told him.

"Mine too, sir," Jimmy said.

Rawls just shrugged.

Galloway peered into the night sky. When they'd entered the forest hours before, the sky had been clear, but now a thick bank of clouds rolled in, making it impossible to navigate by the stars. He backed away from Cargill and Rawls and slowly made his way to where Jimmy and Adelson were standing guard over the Germans, who were now shaking from the cold.

"Listen," he said. "Stay sharp, OK? Things are heading south. Anything can happen out here."

"It's this place," Adelson said. "It don't feel right. It don't feel right at all."

Galloway wanted to reassure the young Mississippian that everything was all right, but the truth was, he'd felt the same way not too long after the squad had entered the forest. As a boy, he'd spent many nights deep in the woods with his father and grandfather, but the nights never seemed as dark as this one. Galloway thought again of the Germans who had entered the forest, but never come out. *You could accuse the Germans of a lot of things, but shoddy soldiering isn't one of them*, he told himself. *They ran into someone in here that overpowered them. Or something.*

"I don't like it," Jimmy said.

"Don't like what?" Galloway asked.

"First, the truck dies for no good reason. And the radio along with it. Then our compasses go haywire. Doesn't that strike you as weird?"

"I thought you didn't believe in ghosts."

"Cut the crap, Tom. I asked you a question."

Galloway patted his friend's shoulder. "Come on. Take it easy, Jimmy."

"Maybe the old man as right."

"Look, it's gonna be OK. The prisoners are secured. They can't do anything."

Jimmy's gaze went to where Cargill, Rawls and Blatty were standing. "It's not the Krauts I'm worried about," he said under his breath.

Just then, Rawls turned and glared at them. If he hadn't known any better, Galloway might have sworn the sergeant heard them.

"Just keep it together, OK, Jimmy? I'm counting on you." He playfully slapped the back of Cole's helmet. "You hear me? Keep it together."

Cole locked eyes with his friend. "Yeah. Yeah, I hear ya."

They broke apart just in time to see Rawls approaching.

"When you two are done eye fucking each other, the Lieutenant wants you to set up a perimeter. We're stopping for the night." He jabbed a finger at Cole. "You got first watch, stumpy."

He turned and stomped back the Lieutenant.

"I hate it when he calls me that."

"That's because it's true."

"Asshole." Cole punched him in the arm and headed off to start his watch.

Galloway turned to Adelson and said, "Well, Addy, why don't we get started on that letter to your gal?"

"Yes, sir."

Still standing up, they both leaned against the same tree. Adelson pulled out some paper and a pencil and looked at Galloway, who just lit a cigarette. Galloway closed his eyes and pushed smoke out through his mouth and nostrils. When he was done, he mashed the butt against the tree.

"OK, what do you want to say to her this time?"

"How much I miss her and love her."

"No no no, you already said that in the last five letters. You have to keep it fresh if you want this girl to stay interested in you." He thought for a moment. "OK. Write this down. 'Dear Betty' – or no, better yet, say, 'My Darling Betty...'"

"Hey, that's good, Corporal!"

"Are you writing?"

"Yeah."

"OK. 'My Darling Betty. Military regulations forbid me from telling you exactly where I am right now, but today we passed through some of the prettiest country I've ever laid eyes on. I only wish we were at peace and you were here with me to share it.' You getting this, Adelson? These are gems I'm giving you here."

"Yes, sir!" He scribbled down Galloway's words, but then stopped midstream. "Sir, this doesn't sound like me."

"You want this girl to wait for you or not?"

"Yeah, of course."

"Then we don't want it to sound like you."

Adelson thought about that. "You're right. What else should I say?"

Galloway cut himself off when he heard the sound of fast-approaching feet and put his finger on his rifle's trigger. Adelson dropped the pencil and paper and did the same.

Blatty pulled up short and threw his hands in the air when he saw the leveled rifles . "Whoa! Watch it, Galloway!"

Galloway lowered his rifle and gave Blatty a hard shove. "What the hell're you thinking, rushing up on us like that in the middle of the night? You want to get yourself shot?"

"Cole found something."

Galloway looked past the corporal. "Where is he?" He grabbed Blatty then. "Is Jimmy OK?"

Blatty pulled loose of Galloway. "He's about a quarter of a klick that way," he said, pointing. "With the sarge and the lieutenant." His voice dropped. "Think he found those Germans."

"Stay here with Adelson and keep an eye on those prisoners. And keep a lid on this. I don't want those guys finding out a bunch of their buddies are dead. There might be trouble if they do."

Galloway gave Blatty a hard look to drive the point home, then walked off without giving him a chance to argue. As he walked, he noticed the mist on the ground seemed to have gotten thicker, hiding the exposed tree roots and the muddy forest floor from view. He shook his head. *We should've listened to the old man.*

A few minutes later, he spotted Jimmy, Rawls and Cargill standing in what looked like a depression in the ground.

"Blatty says you found something?" he asked when he reached them.

Rawls face was smeared with a malicious grin. "Oh, we found somethin'."

Galloway glanced past the three men. He'd been right about the downward slope of the ground, but it was more than a mere depression. It was actually a sunken road and in it were the bodies of six German soldiers. Two were face down, two on their backs, one slumped upright against the edge of the road and the last on his side. A few had their weapons in dead hands, though several machine guns and rifles lay strewn about the road in haphazard fashion.

"Looks like it was a hell of a fight," Galloway said. "Any sign of GIs?"

"Nope," Rawls said.

"Partisans?"

The sergeant shook his head.

"Well, did anyone get a closer look?"

"Not yet," Cargill said. "We were just about to take that look."

"May I, sir?"

The lieutenant nodded. "Be my guest."

Galloway walked down into the sunken road, a gradual slope of about five feet, and went from one body to another, giving each a cursory glance to make sure they were dead. On his way back to the others, he stopped at each body and knelt on one knee to see better in the darkness. Most of them died from gunshots, but the one slumped upright against the side of the road looked like he'd been bludgeoned to death. The left side of his head was caved in just above the brow, and the man had died with a look of complete and utter surprise on his face, as if he couldn't believe what had just happened to him. The perpetrator looked to be the last man Galloway examined. A large, bloodstained rock in sat in one hand and a knife stuck hilt stuck out if his chest. It was this last body that gave Galloway pause.

"Lieutenant? You'd better come look at this."

"I am looking."

"No, I mean you better come closer and look at this."

Cargill harrumphed. "What is it, corporal?"

Galloway pointed. "The knife, sir. That's standard German infantry issue. See the swastika on the end?" He looked into Cargill's eyes. His voice was low and chilly when he spoke next. "These men killed each other."

After the initial shock of discovering what the Germans had done to one another wore off, Cargill ordered Galloway and Cole to search each body for anything Intelligence might find valuable. They turned up nothing except each soldiers' identification papers and an assortment of letters, photos and keepsakes to and from mothers and fathers, brothers and sisters and, of course, sweethearts back in Germany. The same things, Galloway noted as he walked back to camp, that he and his friends carried. Cargill had the perimeter moved back about fifty paces from the sunken road and then set the guard detail. Galloway drew last watch, which gave him the chance to rest for a few hours. Unlike Cole and Adelson, who snored away like motorboats, he found sleep elusive. Finally, he dozed off as darkness gave way to pale, early morning light, but it was a sleep racked by disturbing dreams.

In them, the dead Germans in the sunken road suddenly came to life and approached the camp, moving on all fours like inhuman, predatory animals. Galloway searched for Jimmy and Adelson only to find his friends had abandoned him. His rifle felt much heavier than normal and the trigger was almost impossible to pull. When he finally managed to depress the trigger, the rifle gave a muffled, sluggish retort and expelled a black, viscous fluid from the end of the barrel. The next moment, the Germans were upon him. He tried to run, but found he couldn't move. His legs were anchored to the ground by a thick set of roots. The first German fell on him, and Galloway swung the stock of his rifle at its head. The blow was off-target, and only connected hard enough to knock off the German's helmet. That was when Galloway saw his attacker wasn't a German at all. It was Jimmy. His friend's crazed eyes glowed bright with malice. He fixed a bayonet to the end of his rifle and raised it over his head like Death himself wielding a scythe.

Galloway screamed and was suddenly awake. Dawn had come at last. The first rays of sunlight struggled to break through the thickening mist, giving the forest a gray, ethereal glow. Galloway shivered, unsure whether he did so due to the cold or the terror he'd felt upon waking, a terror that had already begun to give way to a creeping dread in the pit of his stomach. Almost instinctively, he looked to make sure Jimmy and Adelson were still there. They were. His eyes immediately went to where the Germans had been bound and tied to two separate trees the night before. All but one was asleep. The SS captain. His eyes were fixed on Galloway, a thin scar of a smile on his face. Galloway stood up, searched his coat pockets a pack of Lucky Strikes, dug one out, lit it, and puffed away, waiting for the calming effects of the nicotine to wash over him. When he was done, he turned his back on the SS captain and headed toward the edge of the camp where Cargill, Rawls and Blatty slept. He found Rawls already awake sitting on the ground with his back up against a tree.

"You're relieved, sergeant," he said.

Rawls gave him an amused look. "Heard ya cry out a few minutes ago, Galloway. What happened? Cole forget to hold you tight or something last night, send ya off without a goodnight kiss?"

"You're relieved, sergeant. It's my watch now."

Rawls smirked at him and pulled his helmet down over his eyes. "Mind those Germans inna forest don't getcha now while you're standing guard." Then, lifting the helmet back up over his eyes momentarily, he added, his voice hard, "You fall asleep on us, corporal and you'll have my boot up your ass, ya hear?"

Galloway turned and left without answering, shaking his head as he headed back to Cole and Adelson. The young Mississippian was awake.

"Heard you cry out, Corporal," Adelson said.

"Sorry if I woke you, Addy."

"No, sir, I was already awake. Had bad dreams myself." He looked up at Galloway from where he sat with his back to a tree. "Those Germans really kill each other, sir?"

"Looks that way."

"Why would they do that?"

"I don't know."

"Things ain't good."

Galloway knew he couldn't let Adelson see he was worried. He let out a sneer and hoped it didn't sound too forced. "Stop worrying so much. And go back to sleep. It's my watch. You can still get a few hours of rest before the lieutenant has us up and moving again."

"Yes, sir. It's just..."

Galloway waited for him to finish.

Adelson shook his head and looked away.

"Just what?" Galloway prompted him.

"I got this bad feeling, sir. Like I'm not gonna make it outta here alive. I'm scared. Scared of Sergeant Rawls, scared of those Germans, scared I won't ever see Betty again."

He knelt down next to him. "Listen, Addy, you have to buck up now, all right? You can't let the sergeant or the lieutenant hear you talking like this. You could get in trouble. You understand what I'm saying to you? Now, come on, I thought you Mississippi boys were tougher than this."

Adelson nodded as if to reassure Galloway, but the fear was still there in his eyes. To Galloway, the young private looked like a lost little boy who had no business being in the war business. Not knowing what else to do, he patted Adelson on the shoulder.

"Atta boy. Now, get some rest."

Adelson closed his eyes and Galloway watched him, hoping the boy would fall asleep, but he never did. His wiry body remained taut for the next two hours, his fingers wrapped tight around his rifle.

Two hours later, Galloway nudged Jimmy awake with his boot and then walked back over to where Rawls and the others lay sleeping.

"Watch is up, sir," he said to Cargill, who lifted the helmet over his eyes and regarded him with something resembling faint hostility, probably in reaction to having been woken up. "You said you wanted to head out once the morning light was strong."

The lieutenant got to his feet. "So, I did. Sergeant Rawls, gather the men. I've made a decision as to our next move."

"Yes, sir."

Less than five minutes later, they gathered at the edge of the sunken road. The dead Germans remained where the squad found them the night before. Cargill ordered them not to be moved under any circumstances. Galloway thought that was a mistake, feeling it would upset their prisoners, making them more jumpy and a potentially explosive situation even more explosive. He was proved right. As soon as the prisoners saw their fellow Germans, they immediately recoiled, and it took both Jimmy and Adelson to keep them from running away. All except the SS captain. He remained stone-faced and calm, and Galloway wondered if there was anything, that could get under the officer's skin. As it was, the younger Germans' reactions were exactly what Cargill had hoped for. He nodded at Rawls, who stepped up in front of the prisoners, a sinister smile on his face.

"You see that?" he said, jabbing his thumb at the dead soldiers. "You people try to run on us, that's where you're gonna end up. Tits up in a goddam ditch, and don't pretend like you don't understand just what the hell I'm sayin' here because I know you do, each one of ya."

He glared at the prisoners and then stepped back so Cargill could speak.

"All right, men, here's the plan," he began. "Now, I know it seems like we're lost, but I have to believe that this road leads somewhere, most likely out of the forest and back to the main road to Bastogne."

Galloway couldn't believe his ears. "Sir, if I might suggest – "

"Shut the fuck up, corporal," Rawls said. "That's an order."

Galloway ignored Rawls and stepped up to Cargill. He couldn't believe what he'd just heard. "Lieutenant, we don't know where that road leads and there's no evidence whatsoever that it leads out of the forest."

"It must lead somewhere," he reasoned.

"Sir, yes, sir, but that doesn't mean it leads out of here."

"Do you have a better suggestion, corporal?"

"As a matter of fact, I do, sir. It's early morning, so the sun's still in the east. Now look, our first bearing was that stream, which was due north of where we entered the forest. We know we missed it, but we couldn't have missed it by that much. If we keep the sun on our left, we'll know we're heading south and we should run into the stream within an hour or two. Then we can navigate back to the road from there."

"We're taking this road here and that's final."

"Sir, please – "

Rawls intervened then. "That's enough, Corporal. Get the prisoners and your men ready to leave. Now."

"Lieutenant–"

20

"Move, Corporal!" Rawls roared.

It took all the self-control he had not to smash his fist into Rawls' face. He turned and regarded Jimmy and Adelson, then the prisoners and, finally, the sunken road. Something went through him when he looked at it. A shudder, followed by the undeniable feeling there was something at the end of that road, some terrible force that had caused these Germans to turn on one another and commit murder against their sworn comrades, and he didn't want to go anywhere near whatever it was. He took in a deep breath. *Keep it together, Tom. Keep it together. What is it the Brits in London said during the Blitz? Keep calm and carry on.*

He forced himself to meet Rawls' stare and said, his voice even, "Ready to move out when you are, sir." Without waiting for a response, he turned back to Jimmy and Adelson. "Get the prisoners. We're moving out."

They moved the prisoners in front of them and waited for Cargill, Rawls and Blatty to walk down into the sunken road. Then, Jimmy nudged the prisoners to follow with the business end of his rifle. They took a few steps and then hesitated. Jimmy frowned and gestured at them to move down into the depression. They still refused to move, their eyes reminding Galloway of the look panicking horses make when they're forced into close quarters. Suddenly, Rawls snarled and bashed the butt of his rifle into the back of one of the German boys, a look of hatred in his eyes.

"Hit the fucking road, you Kraut bastards!"

One of the other prisoners let loose with a stream of protests in German that only served to enrage the sergeant even more.

"You shut up!" he cried, kicking the German in the stomach. "You shut the fuck up with that disgusting pig French shit and move! Move, I said! Move, goddamit!"

The German was bent over, struggling for breath. He looked up at Rawls with burning eyes. "Sie amerikanische Schwein!"

Suddenly, the SS captain began bellowing orders at the boy on the ground, catching both the prisoners and their American captors by complete surprise. When he didn't immediately move, the officer kicked dirt and wet leaves at him.

"Schnelle! Schnelle!" the SS man yelled.

The young soldier, who couldn't have been more than a year or two older than Adelson, quickly got to his feet.

The SS captain faced the other prisoners. "Sie sind Soldaten der Wehrmacht und Sie werden wie es!" When he was done yelling, he stared at Rawls and Cargill.

"So, he *can* speak," Rawls said to Cargill. "Good. They're gonna love you down at Intelligence. What the hell was he chirping about, Galloway?"

"He told them they're soldiers in the German Army and they better start acting like it."

"My kinda soldier," Rawls commented, his voice laced with a combination of admiration and derision. "All right, move out, people!"

They started down into the sunken road.

Jimmy, who'd been walking in front of Adelson and Galloway, dropped back alongside his friend so he could talk to him. "The lieutenant's fucking up taking us down this road, Tom."

"That's not the half of it. He shouldn't be letting Rawls mistreat the prisoners that way."

Jimmy gave Galloway a dismissive wave. "Fuck them, who cares?"

"I care. And so should you."

"Bullshit. They're Krauts. They got it coming."

Galloway pulled Jimmy aside. "Don't you see what's going on here? This situation is about to blow out of control and we're stuck in the middle of it."

"Hey, we're the ones with the guns, not them."

"Do you know how stupid you sound?" Galloway said. "You ever hear of the Third Geneva Convention? Anything happens to those Germans and we could be brought up on charges."

"Watch who you're callin' stupid, Tom. All I wanna do is make it out of here alive and in one goddam piece."

"That's all any of us want. But what's the point of surviving this mess if they ship us back home and we end up spending the next twenty years in a military prison?" He started walking again. "I'd like to make it out of here in one piece too. I'd also like to make it out with my soul intact."

"I left my soul on Omaha Beach, Tom."

The finality and sadness of his words choked off any further argument from Galloway. Cole turned and followed the other men down deeper into the sunken road.

Galloway watched in stunned silence. *I've never heard him talk that way before. Never. Not after Normandy. Not after Aachen. Not even after Bastogne.* He gazed up past the jagged, ugly tree tops and into the sky. The ghostly, washed-out color sapped the strength from him. No, worse than that. It made him feel weary. And he'd seen that same weariness in Jimmy's eyes just now. *What IS IT about this place?* He gathered his coat as though it could shield him from the tightening grip the forest had on him and his friends, and then continued down into the sunken road, truly afraid now of what might lie ahead.

Hours passed. Morning gave way to noon, and noon gave way to mid-day. The squad moved in almost near silence, never deviating from the sunken road, which wound its way through the ever thickening forest with each step the soldiers took. *We should have been out of here by now,* Galloway thought. He looked at the other mens' eyes and saw they were thinking the same thing. Finally, when night cast its hard shadow through the trees, the lieutenant called a halt to the march and told them to set up another perimeter and watch details. The Germans were once more bound and tied to a tree and left to shiver in their spring uniforms. Then, the squad settled into a small circular area with good cover and dug into their C-rations. When he was finished, Galloway lit his second-to-last Lucky Strike and started to stomp away from the camp, too angry to listen to the lieutenant drone on about how much progress the squad had made that day.

Rawls shook his head at Galloway stomping off and shoveled a giant glob of canned meat into his gullet. He smiled while chewing and said, "Guy thinks just cos he speaks fifteen languages he's better n' the rest of us. Got no respect for rank either, lemme tell you."

"That's not true, Rawls. It's *your* rank I don't respect."

Rawls threw the can of meat aside. His hand went to the knife in his boot.

Galloway fingered the trigger on his Springfield and glared at Rawls, his eyes daring the sergeant to pull his weapon.

"That's enough!" Cargill roared, getting to his feet. "You want first watch, Galloway? You got it. And rest assured that my first order of business when I get back will be to have you brought up on charges for insubordination."

"Like I give a shit, Lieutenant."

"Get the hell out of my sight, Galloway! Now!"

Galloway finished his cigarette and then tossed it on the ground at Cargill's feet, watching as the lieutenant's face turned an angry pinkish color. Then, he turned and walked away without saluting, knowing it would drive the protocol-obsessed officer blind with rage. Three hours later, when his watch was done, he made sure to walk unabashed past Cargill and Rawls to where Blatty slept and kick the corporal's heel.

"Your watch, rat fucker," he said while passing.

Blatty looked to Cargill and Rawls to see whether they would say anything, then got to his feet wearing a sour expression when it was clear they couldn't be bothered. He followed Galloway as he made his way to a grove of trees and sat down next to Jimmy and Adelson. Both had their eyes closed. Twenty or so feet away, the prisoners were tied to a tree. Despite the frigid temperature, the three young artillerymen had fallen asleep, but the SS captain remained awake, his demeanor calm and impassive. He ignored Blatty, who took a seat on a rotting tree stump close by. His eyes fixed on the German officer, Galloway took out his pack of Lucky Strikes and smoked his last cigarette. Then, he closed his eyes. When he woke next, it was to the sound of someone screaming. The sound made Galloway think of a wild animal with its leg snagged in a trap with iron teeth baying in pain and begging for mercy.

"What the hell was that?" Jimmy said, reaching for his rifle.

"I think that was the lieutenant." Galloway's eyes immediately went to the tree where the Germans had been bound, but the fog was too dense to see much beyond a few vague shapes. He ran to the prisoners and gasped when he realized one of them was missing. *The SS captain. He escaped. Son of a bitch!*

"The SS man is gone! Where the hell's Blatty?" he yelled. "Adelson, make sure these guys are secure! Don't leave them unguarded, you hear me? Come on, Jimmy, we have to warn the others."

Jimmy followed Galloway's lead into the mist, but it was almost impossible to see more than a few feet in front of them. Galloway held up a hand and brought himself and Jimmy to a stop.

"Why're we stopping?" Jimmy insisted.

"Shut up!" Galloway hissed. "I don't want us giving our position away! That SS man is still out there!"

Jimmy fell silent. A moment later, another cry pierced the night. They passed a small area strewn with the others' gear. It looked like it had been tossed aside in a hurry. Yet another cry echoed through the mist, this one closer, off to the right. The next thing they knew, they were back down in the sunken road where the mist was even thicker. Galloway stopped again and waited. He'd heard someone approaching from behind. His finger instinctively went to the Springfield's trigger. When the shadow fell across Jimmy's eyes, Galloway whirled around and pointed his weapon at the intruder, ready to fire.

Rawls slapped the rifle barrel down. "Get that fucking thing out of my face, Corporal. If I take one, it'll be from the Krauts, not from you."

Don't count on it, you piece of shit. Galloway took a step back though, and swallowed the words in the back of his throat. "The SS captain's loose."

"How the hell did that happen?"

"Ask Blatty. It was his watch."

25

From further down the road, Cargill let out a third cry for help. The three men turned and walked deeper into the mist, coming upon the lieutenant a moment later. He stood over Blatty's prone, unmoving body. Blood covered the corporal from neck to waist.

"His throat's been cut," Cargill said. "He's dead."

Galloway quickly studied the area around Blatty's body. "The SS man must've dragged him from the other side of the camp."

Rawls shook his head. "Stupid son of a bitch probably fell asleep. Y'ask me, he got what was comin' to him if that's the case."

"Yeah, that's great, Rawls. You're all heart, aren't you?" Galloway spat out.

From behind Galloway, Jimmy reminded them, "SS guy's still out there."

Cargill's pale eyes registered shock. "The SS captain's escaped?"

"Yes, sir," Galloway answered.

"I'm holding you personally responsible for this, Corporal," the lieutenant said.

"It was Blatty's watch, sir!" Galloway started. "Blame him, you stupid – " He cut himself off. "The hell with it. We gotta find the prisoner." He nodded at Jimmy. "Come on, let's double back and check on Adelson. If that's all right with you, Lieutenant."

Cargill didn't say anything. He didn't have to. The venom in his eyes said it all.

The four soldiers retraced their steps back to Adelson where they found him standing guard over the three prisoners.

"Didja find that SS man?"

"Do you see him with us, Private?" Rawls grumbled.

"Blatty's dead," Galloway told the young private.

"Oh, sweet Jesus in Heaven," Adelson said, his face crumpling into a pathetic mask of fright. "Oh, sweet Jesus – "

"Shut up, Private, right now." Rawls turned to Cole. "Get those Krauts untied."

Cole frowned.

26

"What're you doing, sergeant?" Cargill asked, equally confused.

"Finding that SS piece of shit, sir." He nodded at Cole. "Do it, Corporal."

While Jimmy started to untie the three boys, Galloway developed a sinking feeling in his stomach. When Rawls turned to him, he wasn't the least bit surprised by what the sergeant said to him next.

"Now you call to that cocksucker and tell 'im he's got thirty seconds to show himself, or we shoot these sons of bitches where they stand."

"Just a minute, sergeant–" Cargill started.

"Sir," Rawls said, "It's the only way. We'll never find that slippery bastard in this pea soup."

The lieutenant backed down.

Rawls turned back to Galloway. "Do it."

He shook his head. "No. I won't do that."

"You'll do it, and you'll do it now."

"No, I won't be a party to this. You'll have to shoot me too, Rawls."

Rawls pulled back the bolt on his Springfield. "If that's what you want…"

Jimmy finished untying the three German boys, whose pale, young faces were ripe with terror. He stepped in between Rawls and Galloway. "Put your rifle down, sarge. I'll handle this." He faced his friend. "Just do it, Tom. C'mon. It's just a coupla Krauts."

Galloway couldn't believe what he had just heard. He didn't know what to say.

"It's war, Tom."

Galloway shook his head. "No, Jimmy. This is murder."

Jimmy exploded. "You saw what he did to Blatty! We gotta get this guy!"

Galloway stepped back, not saying a word.

Rawls, who had been enjoying the prospect of a confrontation between the two friends, shook his head. "Fuck it. I don't need you, Galloway, you fucking coward." He nodded at Adelson. "Get your dumb ass behind me, boy. You too, Cole."

Jimmy and Adelson did as they were told.

Rawls aimed his rifle at the three German boys. All three of them yelped and cowered against the tree.

"That's right, you stupid bastards, yell for him! You know what's gonna happen if he don't show his face, now yell for him!" he screamed.

The three boys, weeping now, held up their hands. One of them begged for his life while the other two screamed, tears pouring down their smooth, dirty cheeks.

"Louder!" Rawls yelled, kicking at one of the boys. "Louder, goddam you!"

"Don't do it, Rawls," Galloway said, but the words barely rose above the level of a whisper.

Cargill joined the quickly formed firing line and raised his weapon, a Thompson submachine gun with an enormous round magazine and thick, ugly muzzle.

"Lieutenant?" Galloway croaked.

Cargill's eyes momentarily went to Galloway when he heard his name, but the lieutenant blinked and let them fall back on the German artillerymen. Seeing their captors' hard stares, the boys fell silent, their noses and cheeks flushed from the cold. The forest became eerily quiet.

"Don't do it," Galloway whispered.

Rawls looked at him, eyes narrowing as he smiled, then back at the Germans.

They opened fire.

When it was done, no one said anything for several minutes. Thin, gray tendrils of smoke floated from the barrel of each weapon. Empty cartridges and magazines lay on the forest floor at their feet amidst a sea of spent shell casings. Galloway stood off to the side, his eyes empty and distant as he tried to digest the enormity of the bloodshed that had just been unleashed.

Adelson was the first to speak. Nodding at the three bodies splayed against the tree roots, he asked, "They dead, sergeant? We kill 'em?"

Rawls tapped each of the boys with the toe of his boot. One of them gave a slight stir. His left eye cracked open just enough to reveal an eight-ball hemorrhage surrounding a light blue iris.

"Oh, Lord, he ain't dead, Sergeant!" Adelson yelped.

"He will be," Rawls said, wearing a sadistic grin. "Just give 'im a minute or two."

"Jesus Christ, Rawls," Galloway said. "Finish him, for God's sake."

"You finish him, Corporal."

Galloway shook his head, knowing to do as Rawls said would open him up to murder charges too. He looked at the dying boy lying on the ground. There was still a glimmer of light in his one good eye, a light that cried out in unimaginable pain. He'd seen the same look in the eyes of his dying friends on the beaches of Normandy and in the foxholes during the Siege of Bastogne. The corners of his eyes spilling over with tears, he pulled back the bolt on his Springfield, placed the barrel at the side of the German boy's head and fired. The forest echoed with the deafening roar of the rifle shot and the boy slumped over, finally dead. Galloway lowered his rifle and then leveled a withering stare at the rest of the squad.

"You're animals," he said, his eyes falling on Jimmy and Adelson. "All of you."

"Spare us, Corporal," Rawls said. He nodded at the other men. "We'll form a new perimeter around the main camp. No one sleeps till we find the SS man."

The four of them turned and moved like tired shadows through the mist back toward the camp, leaving Galloway alone with the three corpses. He remained standing in the same spot for a long while, unable to take his eyes off the dead German boys. A hazy mist had already formed around them, as if the forest were claiming them for its own, obscuring their young faces and the open-eyed stares of the dead. Galloway suddenly felt like the forest and the fog were closing in, suffocating, sucking the life out of him. For a brief moment, he felt a powerful urge to find and rejoin the squad before the forest took him too, but he knew he was no longer really part of it, that its members were no longer his comrades. He turned and looked back at the way they'd come that day. The sunken road snaked through the trees like a muddy trench in the earth, worn down by the long passage of immeasurable time.

I could lose them if I leave now. They'd never find me. The mist and the night would cover my tracks. If I get lucky, I might be able to find my way out of this godforsaken place. He thought of the old man in the farmhouse then, and, just for a moment, pictured himself emerging from the forest and seeing the warm, orange glow of the old man's hearth through the house's front window. He imagined walking up to the farmhouse through a soft layer of fresh, powdery snow and knocking on the door. The old man would open the door, a barely perceptible smile on his cracked and wrinkled face, and say, "Come in. I'm glad you're safe. Come in." The warmth of the fire would feel good, even from where he stood at the door, and then he would go in, sit down in a soft chair and close his eyes and feel safe for the first time since he'd left home for the war.

"Corporal Galloway?"

The sound of his name being spoken brought Galloway back to the cold, gray starkness of the forest.

"Sir?"

The 'sir' revealed the owner of the voice as Adelson.

Galloway turned. "What do you want?"

"Sergeant Rawls wants everyone at the main camp. He sent me back to get you."

"I guess the lieutenant's given up any pretense of running things now."

"Huh? I don't know what you mean, sir. What's pretense?"

"Of course you don't know what it means, you dumb hick," Galloway said, turning from the sunken road and the way back. "You don't know much of anything."

Adelson recoiled at Galloway's unexpected verbal assault. "Are you mad at me, Corporal?"

"Am I –" Galloway shook his head. "Jesus H. Christ, Adelson. Are you really that fucking dumb? You really think your biggest problem is whether I'm mad at you?"

Adelson opened his mouth to say something, but couldn't find the words.

"Do you have any idea what's going to happen when we get home? If we get home? Let me tell you. We're all going to prison for what we did to those Germans. For good." He dug into Adelson's front pocket and pulled out the letter he'd helped the boy write the night before, the very sight of it fueling his rage. "You see this? You can forget this. You can forget Betty. You're never going to see her again. And even if we get away with it, which we won't, she won't want to see you. You're a murderer, Addy. You think she's going to want anything to do with you when word of this gets out? You killed those boys. You and Jimmy and Rawls and Cargill killed those boys and I"–his voice started to break–"I didn't stop you." He tore the letter in half, then in half again and threw it in Adelson's face.

"Don't do that!" the boy cried out. He fell to his knees and started to gather the torn bits of letter. "It was the sergeant! He made us!"

A voice in the back of his head told Galloway, *Stop, he's had enough. Leave him alone.* But he didn't listen. The boy's protests only further enraged him. "No one made you do anything, Adelson. You're weak. You're weak and stupid and now you're going to burn."

"I ain't gonna burn!" Tears formed in his eyes. "I wanna go home! I wanna see my mama! I wanna see Betty! I ain't gonna burn! I ain't!"

Galloway turned and left Adelson crying in the mud, tiny pieces of the torn up letter to Betty balled up in his fists. A few moments later, he reached the main camp where he found the others reloading their weapons and gathering up their gear.

"Where's Adelson?" Rawls demanded.

Galloway ignored him and walked through the camp toward the

sunken road.

"I asked you a question, Corporal!"

Galloway turned on the sergeant and pointed his Springfield at him. Its barrel hung just inches from his face. "Say something else, Rawls. Just say something else."

"What're you gonna do, Corporal?"

"I'm going to shoot you, Rawls. I'm going to shoot you where you stand, just like you did to those Germans. Then I'm going to walk down that goddam road and hope to God I find a way out of this place. But first, I'm going to shoot you, because I can't stand the thought of listening to another word escape from that gaping maw you call a mouth."

Rawls gave him a sly smile. "You don't have the stones, Galloway."

Galloway pulled back the bolt on his rifle. "Yes, I do. I do because I don't care what happens anymore. When the Army finds out what happened here, we're all going to prison, maybe even the gallows, so what's one more body, huh? Tell me, Rawls, what's one more goddam body?"

For the first time since Galloway had known him, fear registered in Rawls' eyes. He smiled at him. "Yeah, got the old adrenalin running now, don't I, Sergeant? I guess I've got your fucking attention now, you stupid son of a bitch." He let out a scornful laugh. "How's it feel, Rawls? Come on, tell me how it feels. Tell me –"

A shot rang out from somewhere behind them then – the familiar, single booming report of a Springfield rifle – cutting Galloway's rant off mid-sentence.

"That was Adelson," Jimmy said. "He must've found the SS man! Come on!"

Out of the corner of his eye, Galloway watched Jimmy and Cargill run back the way he'd just come. His Springfield was still pointed at Rawls' face, but the sound of Adelson's rifle shot, coupled with a nagging sense that something terrible had just happened, somehow short-circuited Galloway's rage. The dangerous, dogged determination in

32

his eyes moments before began to flicker and die.

Rawls recognized it instantly. "You ain't gonna shoot. You ain't gonna shoot 'cos you're still stupid enough to think there's some difference between you and me." He placed his hand on the Springfield's barrel and pushed it down. "You shoulda taken the chance when you had it. 'Cos now there's no chance you ever make it outta this forest alive. No chance."

"I know." He sighed. "I know that, Sergeant."

Rawls gave him a cryptic look, then raised his own weapon. "Get moving."

He started walking. A moment later, Galloway heard Jimmy cry out, and his suspicions concerning the rifle shot were confirmed. When he reached the spot where the Germans had been shot, he found exactly what he'd been expecting – Adelson had put the barrel of his Springfield in his mouth and pulled the trigger because he knew what Galloway had told him was true – that one way or another, he was going to burn, and there was nothing anyone could do to stop it.

"What did you say to him?" Jimmy demanded venomously.

"I told him the truth, that's all," Galloway replied, studying the area where Adelson had fallen. Something wasn't quite right about it, but he couldn't figure out exactly what it was, especially with Jimmy shouting at him. *Something's missing…*

"The truth? The *truth*? The truth about what? He was just a stupid kid, Tom!"

Rawls snickered. "He told him he was gonna hang for what we done, isn't that right, Galloway? That about the size of it?"

Galloway nodded.

His body as taut as barbed wire pulled across a fence post, Jimmy threw down his rifle and balled up his fists.

Galloway saw the blow coming, but didn't do anything to avoid it.

The punch to his stomach brought him to his knees. Jimmy gritted his teeth and kicked him in the ribs, rolling him over in the mud.

He kicked him again in the same spot. "Couldn't keep your goddam mouth shut, could ya?"

Galloway felt a few ribs snap and suddenly found breathing agonizing.

"Yer always so fucking smart!" Another kick. "Always know just what to say!" Another kick, this one to the face. The bridge of Galloway's nose collapsed under the impact of Jimmy's booted toe. Jimmy grabbed his friend by the hair and hauled him through the mud to where Adelson lay. The boy had fallen on top of the three Germans, the back of his head a blown out crater of blood, flesh and bone. "Look what you did! Look at what you did!" He had Galloway by the collar now and pulled him up off the ground. "And for what? For *what?*" he screamed, little bits of spittle striking Galloway in the face. "A coupla goddam Krauts!"

Jimmy threw him aside and picked up his rifle. "I should make you eat this, just like he did."

The sight of the Springfield pointed inches from his face caused something in Galloway's mind to fall into place. He turned away from Jimmy and scanned the area around Adelson's body. *It's not here. It's gone.* He faced the others again and held up a hand, but when he tried to speak he started to choke on his own blood. "Where…"

Jimmy frowned. "The hell's he saying?"

"What the hell do I care?" Rawls said. "Do it, Cole. Finish him. We can tell the Army that the Krauts got 'im."

"Sergeant!" Cargill said. "I won't allow that!"

Rawls laughed. "You're not in charge here anymore, Lieutenant, so shut your goddam yap, ya hear?"

"You can't talk to me that way!" Cargill said, approaching Rawls.

Rawls turned and kicked the lieutenant in the groin. Cargill went down like a drunk tripping over his own feet. "Shut up, ya sack of shit."

"Where… where…" Galloway shook his head, gagged and spat out a mouthful of blood. "Where…"

"He's trying to say something!" Jimmy said.

"Where…" he coughed. "Where…"

"Finish him, Cole!" Rawls egged Jimmy on. "He'll tell everyone what we did! You wanna spend the rest of your life in the stockade? You wanna hang?"

"Sergeant…" Cargill groaned, one of his hands cupping his groin. "I won't allow…"

Rawls turned on the lieutenant. "I told you to shut up." He raised his rifle and fired a single shot, destroying the right side of Cargill's head. The lieutenant slumped over, his left leg twitching once, then twice, before falling still.

"Jesus Christ, you shot the lieutenant!" Jimmy cried.

"Where's his rifle?" Galloway finally got out.

Rawls grabbed Jimmy by the arm. "Finish him, Cole. Finish him or he'll rat you out to the Army. He'll rat us both out. That's how it happens. He makes a deal and gets off and we burn. Is that what you want?"

Jimmy wasn't listening. "What'd he say? Where's *whose* rifle?"

"Where's Adelson's rifle?" Galloway repeated, his voice gaining in strength.

"Don't listen to him, Cole! He's fucking with you! Finish him! Finish him now!"

Galloway could see Jimmy starting to waver under Rawls' verbal onslaught. "But…"

"Finish him!"

Jimmy's eyes were a mixture of fear and confusion.

"Do it!"

He placed the barrel of his rifle to Galloway's left temple. "I'm sorry, Tom. I'm sorry, but I'm not gonna hang over a coupla dead Krauts." He pulled back the bolt on his Springfield and prepared to fire while Rawls looked on with undisguised anticipation and glee.

The sound of the shot caused Galloway to jump and it took a moment for him to realize he was still alive. Jimmy collapsed in a heap, dead by the time he hit the ground. Rawls frowned, momentarily confused, and then peered into the fog in an effort to identify the source of the shot. Seeing the sergeant was distracted, Galloway grabbed the barrel of Jimmy's Springfield and slammed its stock into Rawls' knees. Rawls went down with an anguished cry. His hands instinctively went to his knees in a futile attempt to dull the pain and his rifle fell away, just out of reach. Galloway rose to his knees and bashed the rifle's stock into Rawls' nose. It exploded in a mess of blood and mucus. The sergeant now lay on his back. Forcing himself to ignore the flash of pain in his ribs as he stood, Galloway pointed Jimmy's Springfield at Rawls' head.

Rawls held up a hand. "Mercy, Galloway. Mercy."

"When did you show any?"

"They was… They was… Just a coupla goddam Krauts."

"You were right about one thing, Rawls," he said, pulling back the bolt on Jimmy's rifle.

"Yeah? What's that?"

"You and me? We are the same."

He pulled the trigger. The sergeant did not move again.

As he surveyed the scene, trying to take in the pile of bodies at his feet, Galloway's head started to swim and, within seconds, he found himself back in the mud. *He's still out there. The SS captain. He's still out there.* He tried to locate the rifle that, up until a few moments before, had been firmly in his grasp, but his eyes refused to focus on any one object. *Where is it? Where's the goddam rifle?* He felt around with his hands, and clamped down on an exposed tree root. *That's not it.* From somewhere close by, he made out the sound of heavy booted feet approaching, and he began to feel around more frantically for his weapon. Just as his hand landed on the smoothbore wood of the Springfield's stock, a boot crushed down on his fingers. Galloway winced.

"I am very sorry, Corporal, but I can't allow that," a heavily accented voice echoed from above.

Galloway tried to turn over, but found he was too disoriented to do it without collapsing entirely.

"Let me help you," the voice said.

Galloway felt himself lifted by the arm, dragged several feet and leaned upright against a fallen log. After a few minutes, his vision started to clear and he found himself face to face with the SS officer. He had on Adelson's winter coat.

"You speak English," Galloway said.

"And you speak German, yes? That was you, wasn't it?"

"Yes, that was me." He nodded at the dead German boys lying at the base of the tree. "I'm sorry about your men."

The SS captain shrugged. "Why should their fate be any different from the countless boys who've already died in this war? Or yours and mine for that matter?"

Galloway wiped the last of the blood from his face. "Is that it then? We're all disposable?"

"In this place? Yes, I think so."

"What do you know about this place?"

"I know enough." The SS man's gray eyes contained a haunted, hollow emptiness. "I have become quite familiar with such places. The world, I think, will soon become familiar with them as well. Places haunted by death and despair." He looked into Galloway's eyes, and said as if to clarify, "I served on the Eastern Front until your Allied invasion."

"You…" Galloway started. "You were at one of those camps? The ones we've been hearing about?"

The SS man nodded. "Yes, though the devilry there was man made and more's the pity. This place," he said, looking around, "this place is different. It simply is… evil."

"That's what the old farmer said. We should have listened to him."

"Yes, you should have."

Galloway's eyes narrowed. "How did you escape?"

The SS captain laughed.

"Please," Galloway said. "Tell me."

Still laughing, the German said, "Is it not obvious?"

"Not to me."

"Why, my dear corporal… The forest set me free."

"How… How is that possible?"

"How is it possible your new truck stalled? How is it possible each and every one of your compasses malfunctioned? How can there be a road with no end in such a small patch of forest?"

Galloway considered what the German had just said. "There's no hope then, is there?"

"I am sorry, my friend. There is none. None for such as you and I."

"But the road… We don't know for sure… Maybe it leads somewhere…"

"It leads nowhere. You know this is the truth." He stood, removed the cartridge from the rifle to see how many shots were left. "Two rounds. Perfect."

"You don't have to do this. I tried to help those boys."

"I know you did. And for that, perhaps you will leave this place with your soul intact. That's what you wanted, no? That's what you told your friend."

He looked into the SS man's eyes a final time. "You won't even try for it? Try to get out?"

The despair in the German's voice cut through Galloway like a dull knife. "This forest will never let me go." He raised the Springfield and aimed it at Galloway. "I will be quick, my friend. That much I can do for you."

Galloway closed his eyes.

A booming shot echoed through the forest, followed a moment later by another that sent a murder of crows fleeing from the treetops and into the black, starless skies over the Ardennes. Most flew far to another part of the forest, afraid, but a few – the bolder ones – made only a momentary retreat before settling back in the branches overhanging the sunken road where the mist had begun to part and the eating would be good.

Ambrose Stolliker lives in the Pacific Northwest with his wife and son. He is a former newspaper reporter and magazine writer, and currently works in marketing at a global technology company. His work can be seen in *Ghostlight Magazine*, *Sex and Murder Magazine*, *Hungur Magazine*, *Sanitarium Magazine*, *The Tincture Journal*, and *State of Horror: Louisiana, Volume II*.

Upcoming publications include his story *Reckoning in Spotsylvania*, which will appear in Rampant Loon Media's *Stupefying Stories*; and his novella, *The Death Chute*, which was recently selected for publication by Strigidae Publishing.

The Last Resort

Nick Barton

For Lisa

If I don't talk about it now, I never will.

It was September 18th, 2012 when I found out the truth about The Last Resort.

This is what happened.

Right as Rain

When it rains, it pours. They got that right.

Macy the cat, though, wouldn't let the rain wash away her afternoon pickings. I watched her dart across the shallow puddles, chasing after scraps of food in the hopes to eat the last of our guests' last meals. The rain hammered on the awning above me, and as I gazed at the miserable charcoal sky, I couldn't help thinking it doesn't rain like this without a reason – usually a bad one. And since this is The Last Resort, it's always bad.

You won't find Twilight City on a Wikipedia list of top fifty places to visit in England. Why would you? The only place of interest to any tourist is The Last Resort, and that's the sort of tourist who isn't exactly dancing with butterflies on a clear summer's day. Nobody comes to this hotel to stay the night before a meeting or to wait out a downpour like this.

They come here to die.

Guests check in, order a last meal, (Macy has the rest) and set their affairs in order, then they hit the bed and… *poof! Check out.* It's a sad case of affairs, I know, but you can't tell the guests salvation can be found here.

They're too far gone for that.

Macy glanced up from inside a fallen dustbin, her eyes glittering with interest. I squatted, feeling my joints crack – still beneath the awning – and offered my hand, twiddling my fingers.

"Here, Macy."

She trotted over and bumped her head against my hand, purring in delight. Sometimes I wondered if she knew why some guests didn't finish their meals. She wouldn't care, she was just glad to have something to eat.

The door swung open behind me. Her ears shot up, and I recognized the alarm in her eyes.

"Skiving with the cat again, Henry?"

I looked behind me and saw Al Smith, the concierge, smiling by the door.

Macy wasn't interested in my hand anymore. Her eyes studied Al with either fear or curiosity. It was hard to tell, but I didn't need her to tell me there was something a little off about Al Smith. He's as cocky as they come, and prides himself on believing he is a powerful figure in this place – not to mention his snobbish attitude toward lowly bellboys like me. Well, he didn't exactly have it right as rain, either. The things he had to do for guests would have put off the most steeled, daring of people there is. When someone knows this is their last night on earth, they'll ask to fulfill all sorts of weird fantasies. And Al is the guy to ask.

But the real frightening thing about him was his dislike for me. Why? You wouldn't believe it if I told you now.

"Macy's good company," I said. "Maybe if you said something worth its weight in hair conditioner you burn through maybe I'd listen to you more."

Smack talk wasn't my best skill, but it did the trick. He patted the top of his head like consoling a sad friend, (he was thinning at the top, and with that shock of hair it looked like somebody had dug a hole in search for his brain) and sent me a look of disdain I couldn't help but laugh at.

Al returned fire with news I didn't need.

"Wear that smile in, Old Timer." He felt around in his breast pocket and handed me a note pinched between his fingers. "Carol wants to see you."

The smile fell off my face as I read her curled handwriting.

Forget feeding the cat and get in my office. It's urgent.

I put the note in my jacket pocket and looked at Al smirking at me, and damn did I want to slap it off his face. After flashing my own smile of a team player, I stroked Macy one last time.

"See you in a bit, short stuff." I stood up and faced Al. "Anything else?"

He shook his head, and then kicked forward. A howling meow escaped Macy's meat-flecked lips. There was the clatter of a dustbin and then silence.

I almost started into the alley after her, but I stood still with a new loathing for Al Smith.

"Why?"

He shrugged.

"Cat's got crazy eyes."

You've got crazy eyes, Al. Macy's got beautiful eyes.

I shook my head, thought about bumping his shoulder on my way out, but just walked out. I've worked here for twenty-two years, five of them with Al, and ever since I've wanted to ask him: *Why do you hate me?*

I went to the lift and rode up to the 2nd floor – Carol's office.

The Last Resort's corridors didn't frighten me much anymore. After working here for twenty-two years, you get to know the walls like children, and when you think of them like that, they're easier to deal with. But, the walls framing the long walk to Carol "The Wasp" Kennedy's office always scared me. Buzzing sounds echoed the paintwork like hornets swarming a hive. The yellow paint didn't help my anxiety at all, but she wanted to see me.

I just hoped she wouldn't sting me.

Three knocks and she ripped the door open so fast she could have been standing there, waiting for me.

Her large black eyes darted from left to right.

"You alone?"

I showed my hands as if to say "what do you think?" and nodded.

"Come in, then." She started toward her desk in the corner. The windows beside her streamed with rain, distorting Twilight City's darkening skyline. That charcoal sky was as miserable as ever.

I closed the door and she motioned for me to take a seat. Her hands were splayed along a sheet of paper, and by the way the lines were formatted with the accuracy of an inner-city accountant, it was a guest logbook. When they checked in, had dinner, called room service, and then… checked out.

She took a breath. That unsmiling face always prompted a lump to form in my throat, and there was always a shortage of saliva to send it back down.

"How long have you been here, Dunhurst?"

She always addressed us by surname, and it reminded me of an evil school teacher reading the register.

I adjusted and the leather responded with a squeak. Anybody else would have smiled at the farting sound, but not The Wasp.

But then again, wasps never do. Do they?

"Can I ask why you're asking—"

"A number, Dunhurst."

I cleared my throat.

"Twenty-two years."

She nodded and picked at the corners of the sheet, something you wouldn't catch her doing in her sleep. Catching herself in the act, she stopped and widened her eyes as if stretching them out.

"You know the drill, then?"

I made a face – I couldn't help it. "I know the drill, Carol, yes. I trained in 1990, then a refreshers course in '95, 2000, 2005, and another in 2010. Nothing's changed."

She nodded again and studied the paper, running her finger down the page and tapping a line at the bottom.

"We've got an important guest coming to stay—" She cleared her throat and widened those black eyes again. "Coming to rest with us."

Something was wrong. Carol never told me when people stayed – rested with us. Only expected me to be on call when they did. And I was. I had a beeper Sandra and Kevin bleeped when I was needed.

"Carol, why are you telling me this?"

"Because you're the only one who'll care about him."

I looked at her with a questionable glance, and she answered with that same monotone drone.

"His name is Jake Brentworth."

The lump in my throat bulged twice its size. I swallowed it down and studied Carol's eyes hopeful she had made a mistake.

"Come again?"

The beginnings of a smile teased her lips, but she aligned them with indifference. The Wasp almost coming out to fly.

"Your brother-in-law."

Conflicting emotions left a bloody battle ringing in my ears. I hadn't spoken to my sister since the wedding, and now my brother-in-law, someone I wasn't exactly sharing drinks with every Sunday at the pub, coming to rest with us at The Last Resort?

"I wish I knew about this sooner."

Carol swept her papers together and knocked clinked them against her desk to realign them.

"Twenty-two years of service ought to have taught you differently," she said, filing them in a folder. And she was right. If you came to rest here, it usually meant you decided hours before you arrived – a kneejerk choice. The Last Resort wasn't a place you booked up days in advance.

It wasn't that kind of hotel.

Carol stood, still gathering her things and filing them, as if expecting me to leave. But I was still a little confused.

"So what does this mean, exactly?"

"It means your brother-in-law is your responsibility. He's arriving at two-thirty."

I checked my watch. 2:15pm.

Anger bubbled at the surface, and I may have been an Old Timer – to quote Al Smith – but I was a bellboy. I hauled luggage and opened doors and hailed taxis. Answering Jake's questions came down to Sandra and Kevin, or Al.

"That's not in my job description."

"Family is family," she said.

A sly smile crept along my mouth. I couldn't help it.

"No, that's not the Carol Kennedy I know. You're not apt to do nice things for your own heart."

Because wasps don't have hearts. Do they?

She sucked in a lungful of air that always made the hairs on my neck straighten up. We didn't nickname her The Wasp because she was a pest we couldn't get rid of, but because she was a heartless, sometimes evil, chore of a woman who thought of nothing but progress, work and providing for herself. She valued her employees in the same way wasps valued humans.

Food for the hive.

"Henry." She stood up straight, ready and willing to sting me. "The last time I checked I'm your boss. Your family is waiting."

Jake was barely family. And the last time I checked, Carol was The Wasp. If she told me she was giving money away to charity, I'd ask her the popular sit-com line: who are you, and what have you done with Carol?

But I wish I kept my thoughts to myself.

"What's he paying you?" It was out of my mouth before I could stop it.

"What?"

"How much cash has he left you for this? Why would you lie?"

She slammed her hand against the desk, toppling her waterless plastic cup. "Look, I gave you a job to do. So I suggest you get on and do it. Your brother-in-law is waiting."

"In law," I added.

Her stinger was raised, and I hurried out of her office before it could sting.

46

The memory of our conversation echoed in my mind as I rode the lift back to the lobby. Carol wasn't keen on people seeing her soft side, (if one existed) so maybe – a billion in one shot – she was asking me to stay with Jake so we could reconcile before he checked out? It wasn't entirely out of this world, but I couldn't recall a time when The Wasp did a nice gesture out of the kindness of her own heart.

Then again, wasps never did. Did they?

The doors slid open to reveal the drab, miserable lobby of The Last Resort, reeking of ancient lives and death as always. It was closer to a shoddy B&B than a five star in the hotel family tree, and that wasn't surprising. Guests didn't come here expecting modern décor and gourmet food. They came to a creaky, old, poorly maintained, grey squat of a building to die.

I nodded at Sandra and Kevin tending the reception desk with a smile, and they returned it. I got to thinking they were the best out of the small staff that kept this place alive. They didn't judge, and they were always happy to help. Even with last resorts.

Manning my usual place by the doors, I saw Al standing behind his podium on the other side, twiddling his pen as if remembering the days of his long forgotten drumming career. He did this as he watched rain streak down the glass.

Then Al glanced at me, hoisting his eyebrow in that maddening way of his.

"Nervous?"

I sighed, thinking of poor Macy.

"I'm right as rain."

When I looked at him, he was studying his reflection in the windowpane and touching his hair.

Don't worry, Al. From the front no-one can see that crater in your head.

But I was nervous. I held my hands behind my back, begging them to stop shaking and turned to look at the clock above the reception desk.

2:28pm.

The Arrival of Jake Brentworth

At 2:30pm, a taxi came to a stop outside.

My heart hammered in my ears, but I resumed my position I've been standing for twenty-two years. I took an umbrella from the stand and opened the doors into the rain. The taxi sat parked just beyond the awning. I unfolded my umbrella and pulled the car door open. The tall man stepped out, and for a moment I didn't recognize him. I didn't know if it was the growing afternoon darkness or the rain that gave off the impression, but his face looked one of haunted nightmares and insomnia. The bags under his eyes were bigger than the single case he dragged behind him.

"Jake?" I asked.

He didn't answer, just hauled his bag out of the taxi and retreated beneath the awning.

I shut the car door and waved the taxi off into the downpour. Jake didn't look at me, and it seemed he had forgotten about what happened at the wedding. It should have been me fearful of meeting his eyes. Those three years since our broken communication hadn't done him any good, and although I'd seen worse from guests checking in and checking out, to see it on my own family made me hate my job.

Then again, I never did love my job. Did I?

"Jake, what's—"

"I'm cold," he said.

I nodded and asked to take his bag, but he held on, refusing to give up this ball and chain he dragged about.

There was nothing left but to revert to what got me paid.

"Okay, right this way, sir, and we'll get you checked in."

He followed close behind me like a scared child in a busy shopping centre. I'd normally engage with the guest, you know the sort of thing. Discuss the weather, the menu and bar, and whatnot, but not with Jake. He didn't care about the menu in the same way I didn't care about Al's receding hairline.

As Jake approached the reception desk, I hung back, watching as usual. His black suit seemed to intensify his misery, and with his slumped shoulders and sleepy eyes, he stood and skulked like a sullen teenager. I stole a quick glance at Al who did the same to me. He regarded me with that odd, sinister grin. For years he always looked at me that way, but he had nothing to be jealous about.

Except my hair, of course. At sixty-two and still going strong.

A phone call at his desk demanded his attention.

Someone probably checking out.

Sandra tapped away on her computer while Kevin assembled papers for Jake to fill out. He scribbled his signature in a ragged scrawl.

"Excellent, Mr. Brentworth." She tapped a final key. "You're booked in room thirty-seven." She handed him a key card and Kevin gave him a small brochure of TV listings and things to order on demand. "If you need anything, just call reception or our concierge, Al Smith." She gestured at him talking on the phone. "Have a peaceful night, sir."

Jake muttered a thank you and started for the lift. I joined him, as part of my job description and new assignment from The Wasp.

"Are you sure you don't want me taking your bags, sir?"

He shook his head again. The doors opened and I followed with a fear.

After all, he had the right to be angry.

Silence pervaded the lift as we climbed, but I could feel the memories of the wedding flooding back in both our minds.

"Listen, Jake. I've been told to look after you until you…"

The words wouldn't come, but he knew what I meant.

"That's fine." His voice was strangled with fatigue, not surprising with the luggage his eyes carried.

"It is?"

He nodded. "I wanted to see you."

Shotguns blasted my theories apart. Of course Carol didn't do it out of her own heart. Wasps never did.

"Why would you do that?" Then the words tumbled out, "Listen, I was shit-faced drunk at the wedding. If I could–"

"It's not that," he said.

"Then what?"

He bowed his head, reminding me why he booked a room here in the first place.

"I'm tired, Henry. I'm so bloody tired. I just want to sleep. Forever."

Too Much of a Bad Thing

The lift doors glided open before I could ask anything else. He keyed his door and I followed him inside. Rooms were small in The Last Resort, smaller probably than a Travelodge. The furniture was brown and white, and the wall and floor colours echoed the visually boring shades of brown, beige and grey no-one would colour their rooms with. But it had a TV, and a phone that went to three different lines - reception, concierge's desk, and the kitchen.

And beside the bed, a glass with a pitcher of water, a packet of pills, razorblades, and bleach.

Pick your Last Resort.

Then check out.

Jake drew the curtains, shutting out the rain-streaked view of Twilight City. I'd seen a lot of guests stand by windows, staring at traffic as if it reminded them what they were leaving behind. Only now it occurred to me how dull a view it was. If this was a place of last resort, then why make it so bloody miserable? Then again, if you came here to die, would you want a reason to stay alive? Most checked out within two hours of their stay.

But Jake wasn't one of those guests, and by the way he stood still clutching his case and looking at the room as if it was full of bugs, he was afraid of dying. The scene became so surreal I forgot I had a job to do, but my usual bellboy routine had already fallen into disarray. Just how do I take care of my brother-in-law I wasn't close with to begin with?

50

"Is there anything I can do for you?" Then after a few seconds, I added, "Jake."

He glanced at me with eyes that had seen too much of a bad thing. Whatever demons sat perched on his shoulders dug their claws below skin deep, and I almost considered calling Richard Keyes, the local priest.

"Jake," I said, stepping forward and showing my hands. "You wanted to see me. And even though it's not in my job description, and all employees are told to never ask the question, I've got to ask."

His eyes suggested he knew what question I had loaded and ready to fire.

"Why are you here?"

I expected reticence, but he sat on the bed, sinking into the mattress like a rock in a pond.

"You're right," he said, looking at the curtains. "I did ask you to stay with me." He laughed a nasty weak wheeze that suggested he was in need of a cigarette. "We… we've not spoken much since I married Lisa, have we?"

Guilt poked its head out of the nest it made in the pit of my stomach, as if hopeful to catch anything else rotten enough to feed my conscious. No, we hadn't spoken. Not a word since his wedding.

"This isn't what this is about, right?" I said. "You're not here just to catch up."

He tried to smile but his lips just quivered, as if struggling to handle the strain.

"It's partly why I'm here… I don't know. There's something that's been eating at me for weeks." He leaned forward and rubbed his temples as if warding off an approaching headache. "It's hard for me to say this. Cruel irony, I guess."

I stood by the bathroom door to get a look at his side. His carrying case appeared stuffed to the brim, and I wanted to rip it open, curious and scared of what he'd brought along. Then my brain reminded me of his last words.

"What's cruel irony?"

He laughed out another haggard wheeze.

"You're the one person I need to talk to, but you're also the one person I never talk to."

I didn't laugh like he did, but could appreciate the irony. We never spoke, true. But, if one chat would allow him to drift off this mortal plane in peace, then I could listen.

After all, I had my orders.

Direct from The Wasp.

"I'm not here to rip you a new one about the wedding." He adjusted himself on the bed to look at me, but talked more to the lamp instead. What answers did it hold?

"I never meant to ruin anything."

"But you did." Now he looked at me. "None of us could eat the cake."

That cloud of shame in my own charcoal sky I'd done my best to banish for three years finally burst, letting the rain pour harder than outside.

I told him and Lisa my apology story a thousand times, and by the nine-hundredth and ninety ninth time Lisa heard it, she just about decided to forgive me. Tracy, my wife for thirty years, found the penis of a twenty-nine year old stiffer and longer than mine, and after catching them fucking on the bed we'd shared for those thirty (not all blissful) years, I filed for divorce. I gave the little shit a damn good hiding, of course, but then he went along and pressed charges for assault I managed to dodge by the skin of my teeth. It was a messy deal that was said and done in less than a month, and I still hadn't seen her since. So when it came down to Lisa's wedding, and I saw the bride and groom models on the top of the cake, I just lost it. I drank for most of the attendance at the reception, and had my way with the cake. Drew my wife's name in the icing, imagining it was her grave, and pissed all over the three tiers.

And Jake gave me a damn good hiding.

Now I stood before him like a soul before God, his eyes cold and full of hate at the memory of my shameful display. And for the first time, I think I finally felt truly ashamed of what I did.

And that made my apology the most heartfelt I think it ever was.

"I'm sorry, Jake. Truly."

He nodded.

"I think I can accept your apology, Henry. God help me, I think I can."

Like grease against a stiff lock, Jake appeared to loosen up, but the misery in his eyes remained, and our new reconciliation three years later made what he said afterward a lot easier to say.

"You know Lisa and I split, right?"

I did. She called me in a flood of tears as I heard the squeal of Jake's BMW in the background. They'd been arguing for months after failed attempts at pregnancy. I know what you're thinking. Lisa must be well past child-bearing age, and you might have been right if you thought she was sixty-two like me. No. She was forty-five, and desperate for a kid. But fate, God, or science, said no. None for you.

Anyway, they argued and argued about anything and everything, and finally Jake had enough, and when he smashed his prized amateur table tennis trophy he'd won at fifteen years old against the flat screen, he called it quits. They filed for divorce and it was said and done in a week.

We Dunhursts aren't marriage material, I guess.

"She told me," I answered.

"Everything?"

He leaned forward in the way husbands do when their wives disappear. *Tell me what you* really *think about her new dress.*

"Everything," I said.

"Pregnancy at our age." He shook his head and wheezed again. "That was a long shit left in the rain."

I winced at the image, but mostly just felt bad for Jake. From all the things Lisa told me on that tear-stained night, their marriage never seemed to get a head-start. I pissed on their cake. Their honeymoon was

53

a far cry from what they hoped Thailand might be like, (rainfall and food poisoning was how she described it) and they couldn't conceive. The latter made me sad, but I also had to wonder why they thought they could get a child in the first place. Forty-five isn't the golden age of pregnancy – more like the dark ages.

Jake twisted his wedding ring, and I wondered if Lisa still wore hers.

"Don't beat yourself up about it," I told him. "You tried."

What else could I say?

"Well, everything's gone to shit since the divorce." He stood up and yanked the curtains open with a rattle. The rain-streaked window gleamed the view of a near-dark Twilight City, as if it knew this would be the perfect gloomy atmosphere for a gloomy conversation in a gloomy hotel.

"Jake," I said, somewhat sick of his dawdling. "You've got something to say, and although you did ask me to help you, and my boss told me to, I've still got other things to do."

He bowed his head, but I couldn't tell if it was annoyance or guilt.

"So to quote an old band I like, should I stay or should I go?"

He turned to face me with his lips curled into a smile – a genuine smile.

"Still a Clash City Rocker, Henry?"

"I dabble from time to time." I shrugged. "My hips aren't what they used to be."

His shoulders bobbed up and down – the visual icon of a silent laugh.

"Can you stay for a while?"

I said I could, and once Jake stuffed his hands in his pockets and studied his case as if debating whether or not to open it, the smile disappeared.

"I've been having nightmares ever since the divorce."

"Nightmares?"

He nodded, but that wasn't the surprising part. His eyes screamed night terrors.

"They got worse and worse, and…" He ran a hand through his hair and looked out the window again as if hoping to catch an answer in the traffic. "I haven't slept through the night since I signed the divorce papers. That's why I'm here, Henry. I need to sleep. It's the only way to stop them chasing me."

I studied my brother-in-law with a suspicious look, and the word "chase" made me wonder even more what the hell was in his suitcase.

"Who's chasing you, Jake?"

"The workmen."

Beast of Burden

It's at this point Jake told me about his dreams of workmen clad in faded jeans and white shirts chasing him through cornfields toward scarecrows crucified above empty graves at their feet. At closer inspection, each grave held an item from his past ready for burial. He saw the stopwatch he broke in school and blamed on another kid. In another grave he saw a bunch of unpaid speeding fines – another with old school detention slips. The belt he stole from his dad and whipped him with in his sleep to get his own back after his own painful childhood. A pair of trainers dead in a grave, the laces bloody from a nosebleed. And the prized table tennis trophy.

Endless graves with things inside them, and the scarecrows taunted him with the words:

Bury your past, or become food

When Jake finished his story his fingers trembled so much you'd think he recited a tricky piano piece. The way he told it without so much as a hesitation to work out the fiction set his story in stone.

I licked my lips and gestured at the case.

"Are those the… things in the graves?"

He patted the top of the case as if it was a sleeping dog.

"Most of them," he said. "Things like ancient stopwatches aren't easy to recover."

I chuckled a little at that, and it almost sounded like Jake's wheezing laughter.

"What do you plan to do with it?"

He drew in a breath and rubbed his hands together, no doubt sending second thoughts back home.

"There's a furnace outside, right?"

There was, but I didn't have clearance to use it. That belonged to The Bald Prick.

AKA, Al Smith.

"There is," I said, "but... are you sure this will work?"

He looked up at the ceiling and sighed the last of his patience.

"The scarecrows told me what to do."

I raised my hand. Fingers no longer trembling. "They said *bury* your past."

"And can I bury it here?"

I looked out the window, watching the lights wink through the downpour. The Last Resort stood on a busy street, and the closest patch of grass was twenty minutes away in Brinkley Park.

"Good point," I said.

"We burn it," he said. "But... I can't do it."

I levelled my eyes with his, demanding an answer. "Why not?"

"How, Henry? How am I supposed to do that? Just packing it away was hard enough. It took me days to do it." Tears threatened to break, and for a moment I saw the flash of fear he faced every time he turned out the light every night.

Workmen clad in faded jeans and white shirts.

"Everything I saw in my dreams, at least all the things I could find, are in here." He patted the case again. "I can't bear the idea of doing it myself. I need to sleep, Henry. Forever."

Forever.

And he would. Jake wasn't burning his history purely to catch a well-rested snooze, but to break a curse and ensure the workmen and

56

scarecrows wouldn't follow him in his eternal dreams.

Bury your past, or become food.

We make our own hells in this world, and Jake didn't want his overcrowded any more than it already was.

"So, Henry…" He held out his case for me, looking somewhat like a midwife handing off a newborn baby. "Please?"

Taking the case of nightmares was akin to voicing a promise to a child that the monsters in the wardrobe would go away. If what he was saying was true – and I believed him – then I could get my feet wet for a while.

I took the case. He drew back and sighed, as if finally ridding this beast of burden from his hands.

"Consider us even," he said.

"You mean–"

"The cake with the urine icing," he said with a barely-there smile on his lips. "Yeah. Even-Stevens."

A silence parted the conversation, and part of me didn't want to leave.

Then he said, "Could you stay with me when I… You know."

This I didn't expect, and I realized even with twenty-two years' experience, I knew, I fucking knew I should never stay. Guests check out on their own, and only if they request help, you get Al Smith to call Richard Keyes and he gets his hands dirty.

My words stammered out of my mouth. "Actually, Jake. I probably shouldn't. It's not right for a bellboy to–"

"OK, then. You're fired. Now you're just my brother-in-law."

A heavy sigh escaped my lips. He had me in a way I couldn't explain to The Wasp. If she caught wind of me aiding a guest, no matter who they were, I'd be out on my arse faster than Al Smith could lose his hair.

There was no way out. He came to me for help, and I owed him more than just burning his past in the fire. I couldn't help thinking my shameful display at the wedding was in some way a harbinger for all the pain he and Lisa suffered afterward. Call me superstitious all you like, I don't care. I've been leading guests to their rooms like a prison guard escorting cons to their cells. And it was inside those cells where they begged for penance from their deities, or from themselves. And when Al Smith's beeper went off, he'd take the lift to whatever room said goodbye to the newly departed, and perform the dreadful task of getting rid of the body.

The furnace.

Then the sky.

"Henry?"

I looked at my brother-in-law, and decided what to do.

"I'll be back soon."

He nodded and turned back to the window.

"I'll wait for you."

The Furnace

I wasn't sure what I dreaded most: burning the suitcase or asking Al Smith for help.

Twenty-two years of loyal service and never once had I felt such burdens resting on my shoulders. No, resting wasn't right, clawing below skin deep on my shoulders, just like Jake's demons. And throughout his three years of marriage, I never once knew how much he and Lisa suffered. Come to think of it, I hadn't spoken to her since that tearstained night.

After this was done and I was back home, I'd call her.

The lift doors slid open and for the second time today, the lobby looked as miserable as the charcoal sky. I took a breath and stepped onto the dreary carpet. Kevin wasn't at the desk, but Sandra said hello and I replied with as much joy as I could. But that joy was short-lived as I rounded the pillar and spotted Al's stand vacant.

"Sandra," I turned to face her. She looked up from the computer, a single strand of straw-hair dangled in front of her eye. "Where's Al gone?"

She paused for a moment, then said, "Checking out a guest."

I remembered him taking a call when she checked in Jake. The ins and outs of checking out guests were lost to me, but the concierge before Al was quick at his job. The body was out of the room, into the fire, and up in the sky in less than an hour. Al Smith wasn't apt to crack on with a job and get it done as fast as possible. But there was one thing about him I knew. He treasured that furnace. Treasured it more than an Olympic athlete would treasure a gold medal. And with my brother-in-law staying here, and Al's tendency to stare into my mind in search for secrets, well, I had a right to be paranoid.

Sandra must have seen darkness in my eyes since hers widened with alert.

"What's wrong, Henry?"

I shook my head.

"Nothing. If you see Al, tell him I'm looking for him."

"He'll like that," she called out.

She was right. Al would play games and avoid me just to spite me.

I went through the fire exit in the lobby and opened the doors into the alley.

The rain hadn't stopped.

The Last Resort was a miserable place. The bodies of the dead were burned in the furnace in the cellar of a disused shop at the end of the alley Macy and I took our breaks. Al's beeper would go off, he'd write the death certificate, burn the body, and send it to the sky.

Just another death. Just another night.

Al once told me he liked the alley dirty because it reminded him suicides were dirty people, and they belonged in the bin. His words, not mine. I never thought of it that way. In fact, while writing this tale far away from The Last Resort, I did a lot of thinking. Why I took the job, why I stuck at it for so long even though I knew the miserable business it was, and why it took so long for me to reach the point when I quit. The first one remains unknown to me, and I stuck at it because I liked to think it was a merciful thing to do. If the world had treated them badly, and I was the last friendly face these poor souls saw before they took their final flight upstairs, then I could rest easy knowing I did my part to help. You came to The Last Resort because you had nothing else. And nobody should lessen their desperation with what they thought about suicide.

Why I quit? Well, that's the ghost I'm trying to banish.

Using Jake's case to shield my head from the rain, I ran through Macy's feeding ground, hopping over fallen bins and slipping and sliding on more things than I care to identify.

Beneath the awning of the shop's back door, I rattled the knob and swung it open.

Patches of light blazed along the floor from the small windows like spotlights for dust motes to dance. Melodic water drops echoed from a room beside me, and the whole place stank of stale water. Baked bean cans with dusty tops sat unopened on their shelves, boxes of cleaning products remained untouched, and rolls of toilet paper still waited in their air-tight packaging for bottoms to wipe down. I followed the trails of light and heard distant rattling coming from downstairs. The door stood ajar, and as I closed in, I heard the undeniable sound of the crucible.

I took the stairs slowly, feeling the steps creak like my joints every morning when I skulked to the toilet. Firelight flickered at the bottom, and dancing with the shadows was the figure of Al Smith with a shovel, hauling lumps of coal into the furnace with a maniacal speed that would kill a man my age.

"Al?"

He didn't respond – just kept shovelling and shovelling as if feeding the engine of a dying warship.

He's in a frenzy, I thought. *He shovels any more he's going to bust his heart.*

"Al?"

Still nothing. In the light of the furnace yelling back with roaring flames I could see beads of sweat pooling down his head – his bald spot shining like a beacon. And beside him stood a bin where used body bags

60

were dumped.

It was empty.

With Jake's case still in my hand, I stepped toward Al and touched his shoulder.

"Al?"

The shovel whirled around. I shot back and grabbed the stem.

He would have killed me. If I hadn't–

The shovel slipped out of reach – my grip not that strong after all – and swung again.

This time he hit me.

Let me just explain what I think happened. I was out cold, that much I know, maybe for a minute or two. Whatever the time, it was enough for The Bald Prick to pull open Jake's case of burden and rifle through his things. No doubt convinced these were my secrets I came to burn, but none of them were burnt when I came to. He stood by the fire – far too close – with his shovel standing like a staff, sweat staining his shirt.

I rubbed my cheek. It swelled like a bitch later, but the pain then wasn't that bad. The sort of pain that hits you first with shock, then as you calm down, it throbs so hard you think you've developed a second heartbeat.

"You hit me," I said, for some reason surprised he was capable of such a thing.

"You tried to trick me." He yanked up the open case – the bottom dangling like a broken jaw.

"I didn't try…" I propped myself on my elbows. "I didn't try anything, Al. I need your help."

"And not only that," he continued, as if he hadn't heard me. "You're trespassing." He smiled at me, and when he did, half his face flickered with firelight that gave him a perverse, demonic look. That terrified me.

"Al, just listen. I was trying to find you."

"What this?" he asked, gesturing at Jake's things scattered on the floor.

"What's what?"

He poked his foot against a Barbie doll, and that's when I noticed what was wrong with it. A hole had been drilled in the nether-region that made up Barbie's crotch, and I didn't want to know how this related to Jake's past. But it did. Everything in his case, now on the floor, did.

"Al, that's not mine. None of this is mine."

He bowed down to laugh. Light blinked off his bald spot as he stamped his feet on the ground.

"If I had a quid for every time I heard that from creeps like you, Old Timer. I knew you were hiding stuff from me. I fucking knew it."

He's insane, I thought. *He's as insane as I am old.*

For the first time in my life – forgive the cliché – I was fearful of my life. Al may have been cocky, and he liked to think he had a job of some importance, (god help me, I thought the same thing about my job) but he was still young enough to believe it. He'd proven already he could resort to violence if need be, but there was something else about him. No, there was something else inside that made him act this way. The way he shovelled coal with a maddened look suggested he tried to cover up a dirty deed and reminded me of Edgar Allen Poe's story "The Black Cat". The same insanity that prompted Poe's character was the same insanity I saw radiating off Al's pores. You don't sweat like that unless you're terrified of being found out.

And Al hid something.

"So, Old Timer." He dropped the case and switched the shovel to his other hand, slamming the blade down like planting a flag. "What's with the night crawl to the furnace? You can tell me. After all, we're colleagues."

Playing to his game was the best idea I had. So I went for it.

"You're right, Al. I'm going to stop lying and tell it to you straight. Man to man."

He smiled. I knew he'd like that "man to man" crap.

As if planting a flag into the dirt, he impaled the shovel in the coal and rested his hands on the handle. "I'm listening."

I raised a shaky hand betraying my confidence. "But you need to tell me something. Fairs fair."

His suspicions picked up like satellites picking up movement.

"You think you can trick me again?"

"No," I said. "I saw you shovelling coal in there as if it was going out of style." He glanced back at the furnace, the flames bellowing, *feed me more!* "I was thinking nobody shovels like that without a reason. And there aren't any body bags in the box."

I was right. He glanced around too, as if hoping to contradict me, but he couldn't.

"No." He jabbed a finger at me. "You're trying to trick me. I know what you're like."

"Do you, Al? Because all I see is a man drenched in sweat with a nervous stammer every time I mention the furnace. What the hell were you doing?"

The Bald Prick's lip began to quiver, and right there I knew he had something to say, but not something he was proud of. His look reminded me of Jake when he told me about the scarecrows in the cornfields.

I need to sleep, Henry. Forever.

"Al," I said. "What's wrong with you?"

"I can't tell you," he said. "I can't tell anyone."

I was about to assure him that he could tell me, but he would see through it. We weren't friends, never have been. There was only one thing left to do.

"I've been hiding my brother-in-law's things," I told him. He looked at me with childlike fascination that made me hate him all over again. *You were the kind of kid who tortured insects, weren't you? Probably keyed cars when you grew your first short and curly, too.* "I'm burning his things so he can sleep. Forever."

Al craned his head a bit, trying to study my story. When he said nothing, I continued. "He's come here to die. He told me farm workers chase him toward scarecrows standing by empty graves in his dreams. If I burn his things"-I gestured at the Barbie doll with the drilled hole *down there-*"he can get rid of the nightmares. I believe him. These aren't my things. The only thing I've been hiding from you tonight is this story. I've never once lied to you before, Al. That's the truth."

Al Smith didn't look at me as if I was crazy – anybody else would – instead he looked at me with a sense of understanding, as if we spoke the same secret language.

"This place," he began. "It's a hive. Voices tell me to feed it. Every night they say, *feed me. Feed me. Feed me!*" He rubbed his temple with one hand, the other still on the shovel. "I come down here to feed the furnace. I do it until they tell me enough is enough. It's never enough, Henry." His eyes screamed a tortured look I couldn't bear. If we were friends I might have tried to pat his shoulder, but I didn't dare move. Whatever terrible state of mind the voices of the... hotel, had him in when feeding the furnace; he wasn't out of it just yet. He still had the shovel, and he had already hit me.

"What voices, Al?"

He shook his head, but not in refusal to say. His eyes were closed and he grimaced.

"*It's never ENOUGH!*"

He stepped back, yanked the shovel in the air, like prying the sword from the stone, and flung it like a javelin across the room. It clattered against a row of shelves spilling unused tins all over the floor.

I cringed against the awful sound, and when I opened my eyes again, Al was knelt down with head in hands – almost rocking back and forth. The voices weren't done yet.

Right then I felt a strange unity build from the things that haunted us. I couldn't help thinking the scarecrows in Jake's dreams, Carol's refusal to say why she wanted me to help Jake settle in, and Al's voices demanding to *feed me more* were all connected. There was something strange about the hotel tonight, (or was it the hive?) and I couldn't help thinking if Jake checked out, all would be resolved.

In some way or another.

"Al?" I pulled myself up and, with a fear, squeezed his bony shoulder.

To my thanks, he didn't lash out. "I need your help."

His fingers parted and he looked at me through the slits.

"Help me burn Jake's things, and then we can help see him out," I squeezed a little more, attempting to be a bit like a father. "He wants me with him when he… goes. I'll need your help with the body."

"I can do it by myself," he said.

I shook my head.

"No, you can't. You've sweated away all your strength."

"The voices are so loud." He almost cried in his hands.

"Al." I knelt beside him. "Something tells me my brother-in-law is the key to all of this. So when he goes…"

Al looked at me, his cheeks red with tears cutting through the heat. "They'll stop?"

"I hope so." I squeezed his shoulder again.

Desperation

Jake's things went up in smoke – billowing out of the chimney with the breath of the hive, most likely. Al was drained, leaning on his shovel with head bowed as if he'd been out slaving in the fields. The weird thing was he looked fine in the lobby, radiating with the same brash cockiness I'd come to expect as much as I've come to expect it to rain in summer. Whatever those voices were, they were probably the reason why he regarded me with dislike, feeding false truths. And whatever evil lived in the hotel, (and yes, I did believe it) the dreams of scarecrows in the cornfields, Al's voices demanding more coal, and Carol's voiceless answer all came back to Jake.

All of it.

After the last item burned – the Barbie doll with the drill hole – we left the crucible for the alley. Macy was long gone, no doubt taking shelter in her home somewhere. Rainwater dribbled down a cracked gutter and we cupped our hands to wash the black streaks off our faces. Carol wasn't apt to skulk in the hallways of The Last Resort any more than I was apt to cook a guest's last meal, but we couldn't walk around with coal-smoke eyes. I felt the right side of my face and winced – it had puffed up a little – and that second heartbeat pounded in unison with the mother lode in my chest. I could explain away my face with a lie, but Al was another story. Kevin, Sandra, and I often shared theories about our local concierge, and Al was weird enough for any one of them to be true. If they caught him with that haunted stare on his face, they'd ensure he'd never go anywhere again.

We walked across the fire exit corridor that led to the lobby – the right side of the reception desk – until I stopped him by the doors.

"We can't go in looking like this," I said.

He didn't argue. In fact, Al didn't say anything. For once the cocky attitude took flight and the scared kid underneath came out to play. When I saw him looking like a six year old who had walked into an empty house looking for his mother, I started to think his attitude wasn't his fault, but a gift from his parents who probably didn't–

"Al, you OK?"

He jumped on the spot as if desperate for a piss and pounded his head like a lunatic in an asylum. "Mmmmm! *MMMMM!*" It sounded like he was screaming through a burlap sack.

I grabbed his hands and shook hard. "The voices aren't real. You listening to me? They're not real!"

He stopped *mmmm*-ing and looked at me with giant eyes glistening with new tears. And those eyes screamed *feed me more! Feed me more! Feed me more!*

"One last meal, OK?" I said. "They get one last body, and then it'll be over."

He nodded, still battling the demons in his head, but I didn't know if I was right. I was betting on a wing and prayer that everything would stop when Jake *checked out.* Only now, while trying to stop Al from smashing his brains in with his own fists, did I realize I was probably wrong.

"Kevin and Sandra can't see you like this," I told him. "They'll ask questions."

"Wha… what will you do?"

I sighed. "I'm not sure. I don't look great, but I can lie. I'll talk to them on the other side of the desk so you can head for the stairs."

Al nodded, then grabbed my arm as I made for the door.

"They'll hear it open."

Shit, he was right.

"I'll cough," I said quickly. "I'll have a coughing fit and then you can go."

He raised an eyebrow – the same judgmental one he would hoist when thinking, *really, Old Timer?*

"Just wait for the smoker's cough." I pushed open the door.

Sandra and Kevin looked up immediately, their eyes widened in surprise.

"What the hell happened to your face?" Kevin asked.

I rubbed my swollen cheek and pressed both hands against the desk, letting my exhaustion pour out. *I'm getting too old for this shit.*

"I fell in the alley, didn't I?" I said. "Right on my bloody face."

"Christ, it's swollen like a balloon." Sandra reached to touch it but I drew away.

"Don't, it's sore."

"No shit it's sore," she said in a way a mother would when tending to her kid's grazed knee. "What did you hit it against?"

I looked to the ceiling to play out my thinking. As I did, I slid to the other side of the desk, and only when they were fully turned from the door did I want to cough. But Kevin wasn't turned as much as I wanted. He liked to stand a little at an angle when talking to guests – probably didn't even know he did it – but even if I hacked my lungs out he'd still catch Al slipping through the door.

"Henry?" Sandra pressed.

"Drain pipe," I answered. "Didn't even see it."

Kevin shook his head. "Keep telling Al to clean the alley. He only has about half an hour's work a day. Couldn't hurt him to do a little TLC."

I imagined Al bursting out of the fire door with his shovel in hand ready to bludgeon Kevin into paste. If the voices weren't haunting him, I think he would have.

"You need to get ice on that, Henry," Sandra said, still trying to reach out.

"What I need is—"

It hurt.

"Henry!"

Good Christ, it hurt.

My blown up face thrummed like a heavy bass at a rock concert with every cough. And the more I fake coughed, the more I felt like properly coughing. Its hideous rhythm reminded me of the opening guitar riff to *Iron Maiden*'s "Bring Your Daughter to the Slaughter". I doubled over for the last two shocks, rose, and felt heat lance up my face.

Sandra hurried around the desk and guided me to a nearby tub chair. I turned my head and coughed into my fist as I sank into the leather, my stomach hitching from rock bottom to belly up. Once it passed, I waved Sandra off and tried to stand, then regretted it.

Would you like a head rush to go with your swelling?

"Jesus Christ." Kevin was looking at me now, back fully to the door.

Al had better be upstairs.

"You need to take it easy, Henry. You're falling apart."

I'm only sixty-two, young man. Piping age for a hike or two.

"I'll get some ice from the kitchen." Sandra hurried behind closed doors leaving me in the company of Kevin and his concerned eyes.

"Bloody drain pipe," I said, beating my chest, as if willing my heart on like a sport's coach.

Kevin winced. "Must have whacked it pretty hard."

That prompted a real laugh to bellow out of my mouth, and god that hurt too, but that was good hurt. The kind I used to get after nine to five shifts at a building supply warehouse I worked at in my twenties, and after those days when my legs were aching so bad I thought they'd snap before the first ten yards home, it still felt good. It was the pain you got when you knew you were building muscles.

Except half my face was broken and there was nothing to feel good about.

"I need to check in on Jake," I said, struggling to my feet, but Kevin came over and pushed me back down easy on the chair.

"You're not going anywhere, Henry. Not even the toilet."

"But what if I need to tinkle?" I said with a smile.

"There's a plant pot over there."

I laughed again, but I kept thinking about Jake. How long would he wait? I didn't like Al being alone with him. If those voices were strong enough to delude him into thinking I had something to hide, then what would he do if left alone with the man who could hold the key to stopping them?

Christ. He's your brother-in-law, and you know what Al can do. Just look in the mirror, Old Timer.

The doors swung open and Sandra came over with a pack of ice.

"Here," she said, pressing the glaciers against my swollen cheek.

"Thanks," I said, taking the pack and sinking into a cold, numb haze.

"So what were you doing in the alley?" she asked me once certain I was OK to talk.

I told them my lie about dumping Jake's unwanted things in the dustbins with the bored tone of a man telling the story a thousand times over. But all the while my thoughts were on Al and my brother-in-law alone in the room.

And what I might find when I went up.

Checking Out

Sandra and Kevin finally let me go after I assured them I was OK, which took about a hundred attempts.

"You really ought to lie down, Henry," Kevin said.

I appreciated what he was trying to do, but I'm a grown man and this old goon knows his limits. Besides, my throbbing head was busy flashing evil pictures of what I might find in Jake's room like a flickering movie projector. I took the lift, wishing to god it would hurry up, and staggered down the corridor. The sound of bedsprings squeaked the rhythm of sex from number thirty-two, and I knew the guest arrived alone. That's all I wanted to know.

Only now with my feet on the ground and heart drop-kicking my chest did I want to lie down. I didn't even want to look at my watch to discover the time. It felt impossibly late and ridiculously early all at once.

With fear I knocked on the door in time to my heartbeat.

The slide of the lock pulled back and Al's face peeked out.

He's killed him. The Bald Prick's killed him.

"Al... where's Jake?"

"In the bathroom." He pulled the door open and I rushed in, almost barging him out the way.

I looked around like a man checking his house for intruders. "How was he?"

"Fine." He rubbed his temples again. God, he looked like an extra from *The Walking Dead.*

"Al, talk to me."

"He was just standing by the window," he gestured at the rainy windowpane. "Wasn't even fazed or anything."

I knocked on the bathroom door. "Jake. It's Henry. Are you OK?"

A pause, then he said, "Did you handle the... thing?"

I shouldn't have brought Al here. Jake wasn't in the bathroom to take a pee, he was afraid. Afraid of the man looking like a harbinger of death in the same room as him. Jake pulled down the black curtains of his burdens for me to see, and chances were he wasn't apt to do the same for the walking corpse. But I couldn't let Al go. He may have been striding with death hand in hand, but he was still Al. If I let him go what would the voices say?

He doesn't trust you. Just like I told you, didn't I?

"Jake, Al's OK. He's with me. He helped me with your things."

The toilet flushed and the door creaked open.

"He did?"

Jake looked no worse than before, but the fear twinkled in his eyes like brilliant stars.

"He's just had a rough night. He's not sleeping well. Are you, Al?"

I stared at him to press home my point, but he didn't look at me. His eyes followed the rain streaking lightning-shaped bolts on the windows.

"Are the scarecrows in his dreams, as well?" Jake said.

I didn't know what to do with this information.

"I thought the scarecrows were only in yours?"

He shook his head. "I don't know anymore. That field, Henry. Something about that place, the way it hummed, buzzed, even as if it was alive with bees. There's something out there, something awful. And if I didn't – if you didn't destroy my things, then I'd be there."

"But you won't now?"

He reached his hand through the doorway. "Not if you burned my suitcase."

I touched his hand. Cold to the bone. "They're gone, Jake. All of them."

He sighed with a heavy breath and pulled the door open. "That's a load off— Jesus H, what happened to your face?"

My hand shot up to stroke my swollen cheek. I'd forgotten all about it the moment I stepped inside room thirty seven.

"Tripped over – banged my head on a drainpipe."

He winced. "Looks like it hurts."

I waved his comment aside. "I'll be fine."

Now standing in the silent room, I didn't know what to do next. Guests check out on their own. To say I wanted to be elsewhere was as big an understatement as Al's spreading bald spot.

Jake studied the room and nodded. "It's time to go."

I stared at my brother-in-law and felt tears form. Jake and I weren't close, not by a long shot, but this evening we shared our doubts and miseries like late night pub drunks, and those demonic shadows we helped scare away made us as close as friends. Sort of. Like I told you before, I kept this job because I liked to think I was doing a service. If people were honestly happy with taking their own lives so they could never be miserable again, then that was their choice. And if I could help them feel those brief shots of happiness before they flew away, then that was OK with me.

For the most part.

Jake pushed past me and sat on the edge of the bed regarding the downpour outside with faint interest as if he was watching a show he'd seen a hundred times.

"I've given this so much thought, Henry. Despite how quickly I decided to come here, it was the right thing to do." He twisted his wedding ring, no doubt Lisa was on his mind.

"As long as you're positive, Jake."

He nodded and then glanced at Al, still watching the rainy lightning-shaped bolts. "You sure he's OK with this?"

I should have told him about the tormented voices in Al's head screaming *feed me more*, but I couldn't shift that burden onto him when I'd just helped clear his away. All that mattered was Jake's Last Resort. He couldn't bear to live anymore even with his things up in flames. Without a reason to live, he wanted peace.

I couldn't blame him.

Jake took a bottle of pills from the nightstand.

"We'll stay with you until the end," I said, gesturing at Al, fixed on the window.

Jake's fingers coiled around the bottle. He looked at them with sudden embarrassment. "Can I have a moment? Alone, please."

"We'll come back in five minutes," I said, indicating the door. "Those work fast."

He nodded and thumbed the cap off the bottle, watching it land on the floor.

I guided Al away from the window, but he kept watching the rain as if hypnotized by the stormy patterns it left behind.

"Hey, Henry?"

With one hand on the doorknob, I looked at Jake with glassy eyes, but I didn't wipe away the tears.

"I forgive you."

A tear spilled down my cheek.

"What for?"

"Not just the wedding cake." Thank god he smiled. "But for... for helping. It's not easy, living. I forgive you for helping your guests."

"Even-Stevens?" I said.

He smiled. "Even-Stevens."

"Sleep well, Jake."

Outside, I pressed my head against the closed door. Jake was checking out and I was hopeless to stop it.

I forgive you for helping your guests.

Maybe my job did say what I thought about life. Why else would you work here unless you were in desperate need of money? No, I had money. I just had nothing else going for me. I'm sixty-two and this was an easy job, and like I said, I served a service. But was it enough?

"The storm's coming."

I looked at Al like a teacher staring down a child talking out of turn. He was leaning against the wall beside room thirty-eight with his head in his hands.

"What?"

"A storm's coming, and they'll dig him up. They'll dig everyone up, and they'll see the scarecrows."

My heart picked up the pace, reawakening the second heartbeat in my face. What the hell was he talking about?

"Al, what did you say?"

"It's coming." He started pounding his head again. "They'll take them all. And it'll want to be fed again."

I grabbed his hands just like before.

"Al, what are you saying? Talk to me."

Then he glared at me with a face I wouldn't ever forget: A ten year old afraid to go to sleep because of the monsters hiding beneath his bed.

"He won't ever rest."

I yanked open the door to see Jake Brentworth, my brother-in-law, dead in bed. He took all of them. The empty bottle held in his fist, now a little loosened as if clutching the bottle in the hopes to sleep through whatever awaited in death.

He won't ever rest.

Just what the fuck did that mean?

I looked at Al again, and his eyes were back on the window, now streaking even more bolt-like shapes down the glass as if playing out a lightning storm.

And that's when I felt it. That *humming* again, just like outside Carol's office.

Something about that place, the way it hummed, buzzed, even as if it was alive with bees.

Except it wasn't buzzing.

It was rumbling.

"Al," I said. "Can you feel that?"

His eyes remained on the window, but an outbreak of sweat pooled his forehead, and his knees knocked together – probably in unison to his rumbling heartbeat. Something was coming. Al remained hypnotized by the window, and I froze, too goddamned scared to do anything but watch my lifeless brother-in-law.

Then the rumbling stopped.

And the nightmare started.

The Hive

The air broke apart as if forks of lightning had cut the room into jagged pieces. We weren't in a hotel room anymore, but a dark endless cornfield stretching in all directions. Black-indigo clouds waited overhead emptying their bloated bellies full of rain down upon us. Al stood beside me, shivering so fast he was apt to break into a million pieces.

This is his *dream,* I thought. *This is what Jake saw. The cornfields.*

"OH NO-OH NO-OH NO-OH NO!"

Al pointed ahead, and I saw it. Stalks of corn rattled this way and that, and it wasn't the wind flapping them.

But the workmen clad in faded jeans and white shirts.

Al bashed into my shoulder, vanishing into the cornfield maze. When I took a glance at the men, a flash of lightning revealed their savage faces, waving shovels above them like a protest mob, and what they wanted was us. Just us. I ran after Al along the path he cut through the cornfield. The height of the stalks outgrew me, and I couldn't see anything other than the dark sky. Faint screams echoed in the distance with the awful yells from the men behind me, no doubt catching up.

The cornfields went on and on, and the workmen's yells amplified until they were close enough to whisper. I braved a glance back in time for us to collide, knocking me on my knees. Dusty mud dribbled off my fingers, but what surprised me the most was the rampage of work boots rumbling past, as if they hadn't noticed me.

Were they after Al?

They'll dig everyone up, and they'll see the scarecrows.

I got up, ignoring my pleading heart, and tore through the cornstalks.

The corn stopped.

It was like a gigantic graveyard. Millions of scarecrows looked like war memorial crosses above graves. The workmen had formed a circle around a close grave with a scarecrow crucified above. I closed into a small gap in the circle, but the workmen didn't notice me. That's when I realized I wasn't really there. Whatever it was that took Jake in his sleep, it took anyone else awake in the room, but they were just outsiders, like visitors in a strange new world.

The workmen raised their shovels and brought them down on the dirt, digging with a calm control unlike Al and his maniacal feeding of the crucible. Clods of dirt threw up behind them, and once the grave was dug out, three foot high mounds of mud lied behind each gravedigger.

I peeked closer and saw a—

His wedding ring.

Oh god, it was Jake. Jake was in the grave!

The workmen got on their knees and wiped away the dirt like archaeologists uncovering the edges of a tomb. They didn't uncover a tomb, however, but Jake's suit-clad body stained with dirt. He looked as peaceful as he did when he died, but this awful place made it clear no peace would be found.

Their fingers coiled around his limbs. His eyes flew open.

He won't ever rest.

Lightning forked across the sky, flashing Jake the faces of his tormenters.

Jake's screams were the type you hear from people watching a catastrophe. Real, terrified screams you couldn't recreate. The rumbles of thunder grew louder and louder as the workmen hauled his thrashing body out, exchanging words I couldn't describe. Four of the workmen held Jake lengthways as if holding a marlin, posing for a photo of their latest catch. Except the marlin was my brother-in-law, and he shrieked in terror akin to torture victims.

But that wasn't the scariest thing.

The scarecrow moved.

It came alive in snap-like motions, as if it had been frozen for years. The thing bowed down with a jagged struggle to Jake, and as it raised its straw hat to take a look, I caught sight of its hollowed skull-like eyes as it bared its giant wooden teeth in a morbid snarl.

You are food.

Those were the only words it muttered.

The scarecrow straightened up with those same painful, bone-snapping movements, to stand crucified, until the next person was unearthed.

The workmen carried Jake away, talking in that baby-like language only they understood despite the earth-shattering cries of their latest catch.

"FLEEBA. COYGAH. MMMUNN."

I was too fascinated— morbidly fascinated to care about Al's whereabouts, or when this would end. They set off at a brisk pace for a squat-looking dark silhouette of a building in the distance. A flash of lightning blazed the front-facing wall of the building, spelling the sign standing on the roof in dead lights.

THE HIVE

It wasn't the name that scared me the most, it was the shape of the building. In that brief bolt of light, I caught the same details and miserable shapes that made up The Last Resort. It was identical. There was no question about it, and then the name scared me. The Hive. I thought of the buzzing in the walls outside Carol's office, the buzzing Jake heard, and the rumbling after he died.

And Carol's voiceless answer when I asked why she wanted me to look after Jake.

I had to see what was inside.

They carried him through an arch-like opening, and the rumbling intensified so badly I had to clamp my hands against my ears. *Shut up! Shut up! SHUT UP!*

The building was hollowed out like a cathedral echoing Jake's screams – the same screams the damned howled when falling into hell. The workmen took him through a silky black veil leading deeper into The Hive, and when I followed, I saw her.

There was no question who she was.

Sitting on a throne that looked like it was made of trillions of hexagon-shaped plates, was Carol "The Wasp" Kennedy. She sat waiting like a demonic queen, one leg crossed over the other with her hand touching her chin, as if studying the latest harvest. And that's what it was.

A harvest of the dead to feed the queen.

Like wasps feeding The Hive.

The workmen laid Jake on what might as well have been a sacrificial table – something straight out of an ancient Egyptian myth. She leaned close enough to bite a hole out of him when the most horrific scream out-screamed the rumble in the air.

Carol "The Wasp" Kennedy unleashed a flurry of wasps from her mouth, ears, eyes, every pore of her body, sending them down the throat, ears, eyes, and every pore of *Jake's* body. He writhed and struggled on the table as the evil things ate him from the inside, flowing through his veins like speeding traffic. His screams went on for eternity, and I wondered if this was what hell was like for Dante. Nothing but screaming. The workmen picked him up again and took him through another arch-like opening, out of sight and out of life. But his screams carried down the cathedral halls like a prisoner heading to his torture, begging for penance.

I was alone in the hall with nothing but Carol for company. She didn't see me, like I said, I was just a visitor. As I looked at her, all I saw were the events that await all those who check out of The Last Resort.

Unearthed by workmen clad in faded jeans and white shirts, told your fate by a scarecrow – *You are food* – presented to the Queen of The Hive, fed upon by wasps, then taken into the caverns with all last resorts where your remains are devoured for eternity by more wasps.

I looked at her again, and the answers crystalized in my mind.

The Hive powers Carol in the hotel. She feeds off the most miserable of people who come to The Last Resort, granting them the illusion of rest only to take them to a place where there will be none. Then in the hotel, Carol demands Al with haunting voices to feed the furnace to keep the hotel alive. The same voices she loved to torment him with false ideas about his colleagues. Just for fun. And by the look on her face when she told me about Jake, she needed new bodies to feed upon.

She was starving to death.

I scurried to my feet, kicking the dusty dirt into a sprint, tears streaming down my face – Jake's screams ringing in my ears, my heart pleading me to stop – until I was back in the cornfield, welcomed by a flash of lightning. Another cluster of workmen had gathered by another grave. Apocalyptic terror rattled my bones as I watched another scarecrow yank his arms back into joint to peer down at another victim.

You are food.

The scream the poor man shrieked made my heart skip a beat.

It was Al Smith.

This is hell. Wherever this is, its hell. It has to be.

The workmen clad in faded jeans and white shirts, clones of the ones who took Jake to his eternal restless place, carried Al like a prized marlin – prized screaming marlin – to The Hive. I slumped on the floor trying to find my breath again as the workmen of death came closer, not seeing me. They passed me for the cathedral, and I heard Al muttering words I couldn't understand, as if he'd inherited the nonexistent baby-language that was local in Carol Kennedy's sub-world.

"UMMMF FUUMMINGAAAA WRUOLLLLLPPPPP!"

The Queen looked at her new harvest, vomited up her new swarm of wasps and the slow, the painfully slow feeding frenzy began until the end of time.

If there ever was such a thing.

I peeked through the arch-like opening and saw the truth, just like I did when I looked at The Wasp.

Al smashed through my shoulder and ran far into the scarecrow graveyard. Another half-circle of workmen were unearthing another grave when Al collided into one of the men. He didn't move, didn't even notice he was there. But Al saw him, saw them all wrench another lost soul out of the grave. That's when his heart beat its last, and then… stopped. Just Al, dead on the ground, his eyes and mouth wide open as if looking at the devil in death.

And he was.

Except she was a Wasp.

Relief came with a network of lightning strikes forking shapes through the sky, breaking the air again. Only this time I awoke in room thirty-seven with Sandra holding my shoulders, and Kevin talking on his phone, speaking words I couldn't understand.

Because I screamed his words into oblivion.

Rest

I've been staying in Twilight Hills for a month now. Nobody's visited in two weeks – Sandra gave up on me. But, after writing about the terrible night at The Last Resort, I know she gave up because I was connected to the destruction of the hotel.

Dr. Hackman – his name always gave me the creeps – read out the *Twilight Journal* as he fed me my morning oatmeal. The Last Resort had blown up one week after I was taken away. I can't remember everything, but the gist of it was the furnace in the empty shop adjacent was left untended. Soon the fire raged out of control and it exploded, taking a giant bite out of The Last Resort. Kevin died there, but Sandra was off sick. All the guests had died too, including Carol "The Wasp" Kennedy and the truth. I just hoped The Hive died too.

I have no idea if Macy survived..

Al's death probably destroyed it. If he couldn't feed the furnace, then the hotel couldn't live, and if the hotel couldn't live, neither could The Hive. God knows how the science behind that works. But that was good enough for me.

Sometimes I think about Jake. I hope he's not suffering anymore, but I doubt it. He was so miserable Carol was able to pick it up like a garbled radio signal and guide him to the hotel with illusions of rest.

But despite the terrible outcome of the hotel, the news story gave me new life. I remembered Dr. Hackman dropping the spoon, splattering oats and milk on his white coat sleeve as he checked my eyes with that torch thing and called for help. They whisked me away for more medical attention, and come another week later I was talking a little, but my physical abilities were fried. One week in a catatonic state, yours would be too. So they fixed me up on this computer thing where I think of what to say and the words print on the screen. That's when Sandra came to visit, but I couldn't bear to talk to her. She reminded me too much about The Last Resort.

I haven't seen her since.

Dr. Hackman asked me all about the hotel, just being a friend I suppose, but I couldn't tell him. If I was going to tell anyone, it wouldn't be him. But there's a ghost in this story that needs to be banished. And I'm doing that.

But I have to tell someone. So please, Dr. Hackman, if you've decided to read this anyway, (I wouldn't be surprised) make sure Lisa reads it, and only Lisa. I'll ensure I note the printout with the appropriate heading.

Anyway, tea's on the way and I'm exhausted. But while I eat roast chicken and all the trimmings with my fellow crazies, I'll smile knowing I've exorcised that ghost I told you about.

And maybe now I can rest.

Forever.

Nick Barton is a 23 year old writer from Yeovil, Somerset in England who doesn't do much else but write. He's been writing since 13, and the very first story he wrote was for a school assignment to write a horror story. Since then he's been working on stories, some novels, but mostly short fiction for both himself and publishing opportunities. He'll write anything from contemporary fiction, science-fiction and horror, but likes to keep stories on the weird side. It's what I like to read, so it's what I like to write.

So far he has two publishing credits to his name. He won the first Yeovil College writing competition in 2014 with a short story called, 'The Strangers We've Become'. And in 2015, an Irish magazine called HeadSpace published his short story, 'The One Thing Hopeful'.

Balloon Animals

Adrian Ludens

Harve Bradley watched events unfold out of the corner of his eye until he could stand it no longer. At last he stood up from his recliner and approached the picture window. "That nitwit who just moved in across the street has as much sense as a shoebox full of dead mice."

His wife, Fran, scowled, her gaze still glued to the television. "Harve! There's no need to be morbid."

Harve's calloused fingers twitched the drapes at the corner of the window like a game show model unveiling a prize showcase. "See for yourself, Fran. He just carted all that junk in and what does he do? Turns around and has a yard sale to get rid of it!"

Fran sighed and rose from her own recliner. She joined her husband at the window. "Do you see anything good?"

Harve's face contorted. "If he doesn't want the stuff, why'd he bother to move it here in the first place?"

Fran conceded his point with a monosyllabellic murmur.

Harve cast another irritated glance at the woman who'd been the love of his life for ten years – and his wife for twice as long. "Guys like him are why this country is going to hell, Francine. Gimme, gimme. Spend, spend. Buy, buy." He scowled. "Everyone thinks they need more of this, more of that. 'Hey, looky here, I got something new! Isn't it fine?' Never stopping to think how much it will cost them – at that moment or in the long run – or if they even need it in the first place. Just one more thing they think they gotta have; and for what? Makes no damn sense to me, I'll tell you that…" Harve's lips never parted to sputter the final word in his diatribe against consumerism. Instead, his eyes widened in disbelief as the man across the street smiled broadly and made an expansive gesture of welcome to the yard sale's most recent arrival - Fran Bradley.

"You bought a TV," Harve said. His eyes moved from Fran's flushed cheeks to her new acquisition.

"It has a plasma screen," she said. "It'll replace that old thing."

Harve followed Fran's contemptuous gaze to the flat screen television they'd purchased a year and a half prior. "How much did it cost you? Never mind! I don't even want to know." He stood, mouth parched with anger. "I'll be in the garage grabbing a beer from the fridge out there."

"Bring a hammer and nails back in with you," Fran said. "You're gonna hang this for me before the late news."

The tab on the can gave a satisfying crack and Harve tipped the can to his lips. After a few moments of distraction, thanks to the beer's icy fizz, his gaze lit on the claw hammer lying on his workbench. He considered taking it inside and smashing the television screen. A vision of a goggle-eyed Fran, aghast at his sudden outburst, drew a bark of laughter. Twin jets of beer shot out of his nostrils, his sinuses burned, and eyes swam with tears.

Harve drained the can's contents and started another.

When Harve reentered his living room he found Fran gone – again. As a dog returns to its vomit so a fool returns to her folly, he thought. He stepped out his front door. If she had gone back to the sale, he intended to go over there and march her right back home. But Fran wasn't anywhere in sight. Despite a miscellany of items, the yard across the street looked deserted. Harve glanced at the setting sun. A stiff breeze had risen, ushering the clouds off-stage at the end of another performance.

After a moment's indecision, he stepped off his stoop and headed across the street. Harve glanced at the motley assortment of tables and boxes shrouded under flapping sheets as he passed. The gathering darkness lent to the fabric of sickly gray pallor of burial shrouds. Harve shivered, but attributed it to the wind. He climbed his new neighbor's steps, looked through the screen door – and stopped dead.

Harve's eyes registered something so foreign that his brain called up a long-distant memory as a point of reference. Fran had once coerced him into taking her to an art museum in the city. She'd spent the bulk of the afternoon dragging him up and down the halls, prattling on about each piece until she had drawn up, breathless, before a painting of a hairy-legged pervert chasing a fat broad through some weeds.

"Isn't it breathtaking?" she had said. "Look at the primal sexuality radiating from Pan, and the Rubenesque curves of the nude woman just out of his reach. What do you suppose he'll do to her if he catches her?" Fran had blushed as she spoke.

Harve had looked at the horns and the hooves of the pursuer and at the ample bosom and hindquarters of the pursued. "He'll prob'ly eat her fat ass," was his response.

Fran went to bed early that night, complaining of a headache – and cramps.

Now, years later, Harve finally saw firsthand what Pan did to the curvy ladies he so wantonly pursued. Fran, naked, writhed and rutted in reckless abandon on the living room floor with…

It occurred to Harve he did not know his neighbor's name. He turned around, searched the mailbox, as if learning the man's name would somehow have bearing, but found only the name of the former occupant. Harve turned back and faced his own reflection in the glass. His double had no answers for him. The descending darkness must have twisted his perceptions because Harve found the man's features remarkably unremarkable. He studied the man's face and realized he wouldn't be able to pick him out of a crowd. It almost seemed as if the stranger was a cipher, a nonentity. So why had Fran taken such a shine to their new neighbor? Her actions shocked Harve. Fran's ivory skin glistened, her limbs seemed unusually pliable. Her partner twisted her from one position to the next with the expertise of a clown manipulating a latex balloon into a variety of animal shapes.

Emasculated, Harve chose flight over fight.

Harve opened his eyes. Deep in his ear canal a tiny foreman rang a bell and two dozen workmen began jackhammering into his brain, intent on reducing it to jelly. He turned his head, and it felt as if the entire bedroom shook with earthquake-like tremors, warning him not to repeat the action. But he had to. He gritted his teeth and rose unsteadily. Harve hadn't made it to bed, and the floor had not been a source of comfort or sympathy. His neck and back cried out in protest as he stood. The beer in the garage, he realized. I went back there. Drank lots of it. All of it. He wondered about Fran. Had she returned home as well?

Deciding to investigate, Harve sagged against the hallway wall and moved, slug-like, toward the living room. Something played on the television, a cooking show, by the sound. Yet when Harve, with the determination of an Everest climber, finally reached his living room, he found both televisions silent. Jagged holes gaped like gigantic gunshot wounds in the centers of both screens. Harve knew at a glance they were beyond repair. The two recliners hunched nearby like overweight detectives surveying a murder scene. Careful to move only his eyes, Harve scanned the room. The size of the holes in the screen made him think of the hammer – Fran's request from the garage. He looked around, but didn't find it.

Harve realized then that the sounds of the 'cooking show' continued. They came from the kitchen. Someone hummed. Bacon fried in a skillet. Its welcoming scent drew him forward. Harve inched into the room. He found Fran – and his hammer.

Fran, facing away from him, stood at the stove flipping fried eggs and bacon with a spatula and hummed an old tune by Neil Diamond. Harve bent and forcibly evacuated the beer from his stomach in three searing contractions. He didn't know which had brought about the involuntary purge; the song sung 'grue' or the hammer, wedged claw-side-first into the back of his wife's skull.

And I was bitching about my headache, Harve thought. Fran noticed him, smiled vacantly, and turned off the burner. She moved the skillet to one of the cool burners and grabbed a wash rag from the sink. Fran knelt, and began to sop up the yellow-brown mess Harve had just made. The wooden handle of the hammer tapped her between the shoulder blades as she worked. Harve dry-heaved his way through the proceedings. He wanted to flee but didn't; he needed to understand.

"Fran, what's happened to you?"

She stood and faced him. "I'm fine."

"But… the hammer." Harve felt helpless.

"Oh, that came after." Fran waved her hand as if to dismiss his concern. "You had too much to drink. This is only my flesh. A shell. There's enough of me here to keep going for a while, to help you with the transition. My body is on autopilot, while my spirit…." She looked away.

"Your spirit, what?" Harve's mouth hung open. He wiped his suddenly-sweaty palms on his shirtfront.

"Nothing." She squared her shoulders as if shaking off lingering doubts. "It's better this way. I prefer it."

The words stung. His wife had been unfaithful and now seemed to be saying that though she'd returned home to him, her heart remained across the street with the stranger.

Harve turned, and lurched back down the hallway.

"I'll cover a plate for you!" Fran's words followed him as he shambled to the door leading to the garage. He flipped the light switch, but the naked overhead bulb's light stabbed at his eyes. Harve swatted the light back off and descended the steps in semi-darkness. His work boot blundered through the landmine that he had set for himself – empty beer cans skittered across the floor in an explosion of sound.

Harve reached his pickup, climbed into the cab. He considered starting the engine, just letting it run. Instead, he sat behind the wheel and wept. After a time, he slept.

The garage wallowed in darkness. Harve wondered about the time, about the day and date, even. He felt a sense of loss, of something taken from him. The world had gone on without him. He wondered what he missed, if he would ever catch up. Then he remembered Fran, the neighbor and the hammer, and his feeling of unease multiplied. He fumbled with the door handle and crawled from the pickup. His headache, he noticed, had diminished. Harve took what comfort he could from this. Fire ants swarmed his legs and he stomped his feet, trying to restore circulation. His bladder complained within him like an over-inflated water balloon.

He made the toilet his first stop. Force of habit took over and he dropped a single square of paper into the water. He unzipped his trousers, took out "the M16" (though Fran, when she learned of his nickname, had suggested "single-shot Derringer" instead) and emptied an entire clip, as it were, onto the wet square. Upon shredding the enemy to his satisfaction, Harve holstered, zipped up, and made his way through the house. He found the kitchen, dining room, and bedroom empty. All cleaned to an immaculate shine since his second sojourn to the garage.

Harve found Fran sitting in the living room. This room had also been put to rights as well, though both televisions remained. "I cleaned the hammer and hung it back up for you," Fran murmured.

"And you picked up my empties." Harve realized he hadn't kicked any cans on his return trip through the garage.

"Yes."

"You did a lot of cleaning."

"I hope that makes you happy. I'm not sure what does anymore."

"How's…" Harve swallowed the lump in his throat. "How's your head, Franny?" His question came out timid and tentative. The pet name was one he hadn't used in years.

"It's fine."

"You should see a doctor."

"Harve, really, it's fine."

An awkward silence fell between them. Harve heard the ticking of the wall clock. A vehicle passed on the street. His stomach rumbled. "Any of that breakfast left?"

Fran nodded. "I cooked you lunch too. It's all there in the fridge."

Harve, not knowing what else to say or do, made his way to the kitchen.

Fran didn't go to sleep. She sat in silence on her recliner, staring into space.

Harve, not the least bit tired after spending the better part of the day sleeping in his truck, sat up with her. Harve watched Fran with a careful eye, mentally tabulating the things she didn't do:

Talk. Move. Blink.

Her breathing was shallow and intermittent. At length she closed her eyes. A contented, peaceful smile softened her features.

Harve watched and waited for as long as he could stand it.

"Fran."

She didn't respond.

"Fran!"

She shuddered in her chair. Harve leapt forward and shook her gently. Her eyelids fluttered open, revealing only whites; her eyes had rolled in their sockets. Harve felt panic creeping in, forcing the sense right out of his brain. Did she need mouth to mouth? The Heimlich? Harve rapped his knuckles against his forehead in frustration. An ambulance. He needed to call an ambulance.

Harve stood, intending to carry out his plan of action. Fran, still in her chair, mumbled something. "Gbye fr nw massr." Harve considered asking her to repeat what she'd said but something stopped him; a delayed deciphering of her garbled words that led him to a thought he didn't care to pursue. Instead, he turned. The phone, hanging on the wall above the dining room table, seemed at least a football field away.

Fran let out a shuddering gasp and Harve paused. Her chest hitched, as if she had begun panting. Then it sounded as if Fran were gargling. The memory of the first – and only other – time Harve had heard the sound clawed its way into his memory like a hand bursting from a freshly-filled grave: the death rattle of his great-grandfather's last breath. Harve, not knowing what else to try, did something he hadn't done in years. He stooped and embraced his wife.

He pulled her limp body forward, tipping her from the chair. Harve patted her back as one comforts a crying child. Fran's breathing steadied, slowed.

"Harve?"

He felt a thrill at the sound of her voice, quiet, but clear.

"Franny. I thought I'd lost you." The hot tears spilling down his cheeks shocked him. He eased his wife back onto her recliner. Her face was still vacant, glassy, an abandoned office building not yet defiled by graffiti and looting. Fran sat as if in a trance. She was back from wherever her mind had gone, but she still wasn't herself.

"Fran…" Harve grasped for words. "Are you all right?"

"Yes." Dreamlike.

"Where… were you?"

Another contented smile dimpled her cheeks. "Master took us all for a walk."

Harve noticed his hands trembled. His life had become a badly-written scene in which he'd been forced to perform. He cast about the room as if some piece of furniture, some nearby prop, would help him discover his next line. A flash of color outside caught his attention. The man across the street was entering his home's front door. The tendons in Harve's knees popped as he lunged to the window. He watched a colorful assortment of floating spheres disappear from view as the door closed.

Harve turned and studied Fran again. His wife seemed barely aware of her surroundings, but not in any pain. He took a modicum of solace from this as he hurried to the garage. Harve had to get her to the hospital. He'd tell the doctor there had been a terrible accident, a brain injury. Harve opened the passenger door and pressed the button on the garage door opener. He meant to return into the house for Fran, but as the door rose a dark figure silhouetted by sunshine hurtled toward him. Instinct kicked in; Harve clenched his fist intending to swing.

"Don't, Harve! It's me!"

Pete Williams, who lived next door, held up his brown hands as if surrendering. He looked like he'd been crying. Harve dropped his hand and listened to what Pete had to say.

The crickets fell silent and Harve mentally cursed them for betraying his position. He glanced at Pete hiding behind the rose bushes on the other side of the stranger's front steps. Pete carried a crowbar. Harve had brought along his hammer as a symbolic and hopefully effective form of intimidation.

Now they crouched in growing darkness. "We're gonna put the fear into him," Pete whispered. Harve had a feeling they each had a different idea of what that meant. Scare tactics? Vandalism? A beating? Harve realized they should have ironed out the details before positioning themselves around the stranger's door.

Pete's wife, Charlene, had come home with a new lamp and a satisfied smirk. Pete complained she'd spent the entire day "quiet as a shirt on a hanger."

The moon overhead illuminated the entire scene. Harve pressed his back against the exterior of the stranger's house. The side of the house still held the heat from the recently-set sun and to Harve the structure felt like a living, breathing thing.

The front door swung open and the stranger emerged. In his right hand he carried at least a dozen floating balloons. He bounded down his front steps and sauntered up the walk. Harve broke from cover and ran after him. "Hey!"

The man turned. "Yes?" His tone resonated strangely in Harve's ears, as if the stranger had flies crawling in his throat, adding their voice to his.

"You got a lotta nerve messing around with our women," Harve said. Pete had also approached, crowbar in hand.

The man with the balloons lashed out with his free hand, connecting with Harve's ample gut. Harve felt the wind explode from his lungs and he collapsed as if struck by lightning.

"This isn't usually my way, but the threat of violence begets violence," the stranger said. Pete circled their adversary, careful to stay out of striking distance.

Harve, feeling helpless as a beached orca, struggled to a crouch. Air trickled into his lungs. The moonlight gave him a good look at the balloons still clenched in the stranger's hand. Inside each inflated orb was a shimmering miasma bearing the features of someone he knew from the neighborhood. The faces swirled and bobbed, and seemed to shriek silently in their iridescent latex prisons. Or were the faces contorted in ecstasy? Harve couldn't tell. He threw his hammer and the stranger stepped aside – right into the path of Pete's swinging crowbar.

Steel connected with skull. The stranger sagged and Pete caught the strings attached to the balloons and wrested them from the other man's grip. The stranger fell to his knees and then pitched forward onto the lawn.

"Pete, wait. What are you going to do?" Harve gazed at the uncanny bouquet.

"I'm going to find the one that has Char's soul inside it and let her loose."

Souls, Harve thought. And the mysterious stranger had been taking them for another walk. Balloon animals; that's all they were to him.

Pete sorted through the uncanny orbs. Harve looked past Pete and his breath caught. Fran stood on their stoop. Next door, Charlene stood near the mailbox. He looked up and down the street. Several other neighbors stood watching. He recognized most of them as visitors to the stranger's sale.

Pete found the balloon he wanted and separated it from the others. Then he handed the rest to Harve and trotted back toward the stranger's house.

"What are you doing?" Harve asked.

"I want my wife to be herself again." Pete held the balloon in his hands. Harve saw the approximation of Charlene's face within the orb contort with terror. Pete apparently didn't notice. He pressed the balloon against the thorny stems and it popped.

An anguished cry rose from all directions. Harve jerked his head to where Charlene had stood. Pete's wife disintegrated before their eyes, dissipating into the night air like smoke. The lamentations came from those enslaved but still living, as if warning them against any further action. Harve looked at Pete, arms at his sides, mouth hanging open in shock.

Aware that grief, perhaps mingled with rage, would soon follow, Harve decided to take the remaining balloons home for safe keeping. He needed to call the police – let them decide how many ambulances to send. Harve began to turn away.

A freight train struck the arm holding the balloons. He heard the bone in his upper arm break, and then a corresponding pain lanced through him.

The stranger swiped at the balloons. "Those are mine! They belong to me." Two more popped as he clutched at them. Harve knew two more souls had been released – but to what fate? Even if they'd escaped the stranger, they were still dead. This hadn't been his intention when he'd agreed to confront their lascivious neighbor. Harve wished they'd tied him up, or killed him.

He turned to look for Fran and the stranger wrested the remaining spheres from his grasp. Harve staggered back. His eyes watered and the stranger swam in and out of focus. Harve tried to identify his wife in the cluster of balloons. "When a bargain has been struck," the stranger droned. "It's a sacred contract no one can–"

"Shut… your… damn….. dirty… mouth!"

Pete punctuated each word with a blow from his crowbar. The stranger sagged then collapsed, this time for good. His hand relaxed and the balloons took flight. Each confined soul rose into the sky on a penultimate journey. Pete dropped to his knees, gasping for breath. Harve did his best to ignore the pain lancing through his arm. It wasn't easy. He ran and leapt, extending his stocky frame as high as he could, the fingertips from his good arm grasping at air...

And then he was falling.

The city held funerals and memorial services for the dead, thirteen in all. Harve attended every one. There were no bodies to bury. The victims simply disappeared when they died. Some went sooner than others. The lingering victims shambled about their somnambulistic routines until one day, or night, their balloons – wherever they'd each ended up – popped. The last person to disintegrate was Maude Atkins – a full week after everyone else had died. Some speculated her balloon had been found and kept intact, at least for a while.

Harve brought a bouquet of flowers and a sympathy card to Pete's house. Pete had a similar gift for Harve and they exchanged their plants and platitudes. The two men shared an awkward silence. Like soldiers who'd survived a brutal battle fought side-by-side, they had no desire to relive it. The men shook hands and parted.

Pete put his home on the market and moved away. A few others in the neighborhood followed suit. A pall lingered over the town. The mysterious stranger disappeared. Some said he'd moved. Others held the opinion he'd been counted among the dead. Even Harve and Pete remained unclear as to what became of their short-term neighbor.

Harve's arm healed, though recovery went slowly. In cold or wet weather his arm ached almost as bad as his head had the morning after the whole nightmare had started. He returned to work at the factory. His boss moved him from the floor to a cushy desk job, and nobody resented Harve for it. He counted this among his blessings.

Two months after that fateful day, Harve took a half-day and returned home from work early. He pulled into the garage, switched off the truck's ignition, closed the garage door, and entered his silent house. Harve prepared a sandwich in the kitchen. Without bothering to turn on the light, he sat at the kitchen table and ate in silence. He shuffled to the living room and retrieved a photo album from the particle-board book case. Fran always had to take pictures. He sank into his recliner and turned the pages. She'd kept her figure, he noted. And she'd kept him happy, warm, fed. Had a mind of her own, but for the life of him, he couldn't recall why that had bothered him so. Harve set aside the photo album before the tears returned. He sat in silence, watching the shadows crawl across the wall. When he felt ready, Harve stood up and walked into the bedroom. He flipped on the light and gazed at his bed – and the figure lying on it.

It was a miracle that the harm he'd done her hadn't been fatal. Harve had examined her wound one morning as she'd slept. The claw end of the hammer had wedged between the parietal and occipital bones of her skull but hadn't penetrated deep enough to damage the brain. Though Harve still struggled with the mysterious man's Svengali-like hold over his wife, he had to admit that whatever gifts the stranger had lent to her had helped her survive.

"Fran, wake up."

Like every other night, the figure stirred.

He was struck again by his wife's straightforward beauty. She stretched languidly. He wiped away a tear – not of sorrow but of gratitude. He seated himself on the edge of the bed and helped her to sit up. Her head lolled.

"Hrv?"

"Yes, Franny, it's me."

"I dnt…"

"Shhh. Wait a moment."

He rose and moved across the room. Harve retrieved an old-fashioned hat box from the top shelf of the closet and sat it on the dresser. Harve lifted the lid and removed a reddish-tinted balloon with the reverence and care of someone handling the world's most delicate and priceless crystal. With efficiency born of careful practice he untied the end of the balloon with extreme care and turned back to his wife.

Fran stared at nothing in particular. Vapid, vacant. He sat beside her again, raising the balloon to her lips. "Just like last time," he murmured. "Take a sip. Careful."

Fran did as instructed while Harve kept a tight hold on each side of the balloon's tip, ensuring restricted air flow. He didn't dare waste any of it.

As she reclaimed a bit of her soul, Fran became more alert, more energetic, more like herself. Harve retied the end of the balloon – he'd practiced on regular inflated balloons before daring to try on hers – and placed it back in the hatbox. This he reverently returned to its high shelf.

"Oh, you're home! And I've been napping. Shall I get started on

96

supper?" Fran asked. "House cleaning? Love making?" Her impish smile made her look ten years younger. Harve swallowed the lump in his throat. He knew it wouldn't last. The clarity would fade. Soon she'd be lost to him again. She would forget about him, lose her ability to communicate, and fall back into the mysterious wasteland the stranger had left in her mind. He was too frightened to let her inhale the entire contents in one session. What if the clarity didn't last? What if he squandered her most precious resource? What then? Harve also knew that one day – far too soon, he feared – her balloon would run out of air. He cursed the stranger who had moved into the neighborhood and stolen his wife away.

"Just take it easy, okay Franny?" The memory of his wife and the stranger entwined on the floor rose in his mind but he pushed the thought away.

"Are you sure you don't want me to fry you a burger? Maybe heat up some veggies?" She beamed up at him. "Maybe go for a walk or do some yard work? Or do you want to watch some television?"

Harve winced and shook his head. He didn't even want to waste the time it would take to explain that the TVs had never been replaced. Harve reached out to stroke his wife's arm instead. Then he leaned in to plant a soft kiss on her warm cheek.

"I want to hold you, Franny. I just want to hold you close."

Adrian Ludens is a radio announcer and dark fiction author from Rapid City, South Dakota. His newest collection, When Bedbugs Bite, is available on Amazon in paperback and Kindle formats. Other recent publication appearances include: Shadows Over Main Street, Now Playing in Theater B, Abstract Jam #3, Body Parts #6, and The Mammoth Book of Jack the Ripper Stories. Adrian is a fan of hockey, horror fiction, heavy metal, and exploring abandoned buildings.

The Absent Hand

Colin Hinckley

One morning I woke up and my left hand was gone. Not severed, not cut; no blood on the sheets, no viscera to be seen. Just a smooth stump and then an absence of hand. My first thought, of course, was I experienced a very vivid dream and upon shaking my stump a few times, closing my eyes, and rolling over in bed, I would snap awake and my hand would reappear. But this was not the case. And my hand remains absent.

I did my best to cope with it. I pored over medical texts and ancient ritualistic tomes, plumbed the depths of the Internet and even ruminated over religious works, but no plausible explanation presented itself to me. I went to my doctor, Dr. Amleth, who seemed utterly stymied and gave me no helpful recourse, save the suggestion of getting a prosthetic, which I did after the recurring questions from acquaintances and strangers alike proved too much for my patience. The prosthetic was a simple, passable beige that more or less matched my skin color. When I was fitted for it, Amleth patted me on the shoulder and assured me he could hardly tell the difference. He smiled, and I knew he was relieved to put the matter behind him. He had been my doctor for years and was always supportive, but the sudden disappearance of my hand had shaken him. It was clear he was not keen to ruminate over it. And so he foisted the prosthetic on me as a sort of panacea and he sent me on my way. The thing itself was useless in the sense that it was merely aesthetic, but invaluable in that it kept me from the incessant gaze and inquiries of those with a more persistent sense of voyeurism. And after some time, a state of normalcy returned.

It wasn't until one evening several months later, as I sat in my living room reading, that I began to reconsider my circumstances. I sat curled in my overstuffed, maroon armchair, a book of drawings by Doré sitting in my lap, when a peculiar sound started emanating from my bedroom. I looked up from the illustration of Betram de Born and frowned toward my doorway. It was a low, pulsating thrumming, similar perhaps to the sound of a didgeridoo, but deeper and certainly more disconcerting. The sound put an alarming ache in the pit of my stomach and for several minutes, I did not move. My hand remained poised over the corner of the page, about to turn; and after a few moments, I realized the stump beneath my latex and plastic replacement was tingling unpleasantly. When I became aware of the sensation, I broke my stasis and undid the clasps holding the prosthetic in place and looked down at the spot where my left hand once was. It looked the same as ever, but the tingling sensation remained. I rubbed it vigorously with my right hand, but it did no good. I looked back in the direction of my room and, gathering my resolve, stood up and began to walk deeper into the pulse.

When I was perhaps three paces away from the entrance to my bedroom, however, the alien sound ceased entirely and the tingling in my stump receded. I stopped walking as it ceased, then vaulted the last three steps through the doorway and flicked the switch. Light filled the space and I scanned the room. Nothing seemed out of place. I practically sprinted past the bed and threw open my closet door before any smidgeon of courage could be dashed by rational thought. But again, nothing seemed out of place, except for the usual disarray of mismatched shoes and rumpled button downs. I turned back around and my eye was drawn to my bed. The sheets were in a twirled and tossed mess and the indentation of my head was still visible on my pillow. I glanced at the bedside table. Something bothered me about the scene, but I couldn't quite put my finger on what exactly was wrong. It was in this moment I decided to get a cat.

In my research of possible explanations on the disappearance of my hand, I had come across various supernatural reasons that seemed unsatisfying. Curses, demons, and poltergeists were all known for causing mischief that wreaked havoc on the human psyche; stealing a hand could be in tune with that sort of behavior. But I came across nothing that convinced me there was any reason I might be the target of such supernatural occurrences. That being said, I had been spooked by the phantom noise in my bedroom, and many of these texts suggested an animal companion could be helpful for both emotional support and in their ability to sense the supernatural more precisely than humans. And being alone in my house had just become a dreadful thought.

The next day I went to the shelter to pick out my new feline companion. There was the usual smattering of older and less appealing cats, some in various states of decrepitude, others newly born and abandoned. The woman at the front desk smiled at me in a sort of strained but kind way I knew meant that she pitied me. A single, middle-aged man seeking companionship from discarded animals because he could not find any from a fellow human. She was not entirely wrong. She led me to the back where a large knee high fence sequestered off a concrete patch of floor filled with cat toys, towels and urine stains. A wall of black wired cages were piled in the back. The cats milled around, playing with each other or napping on soiled towels. The sight gave me a pleasant warmth in my midsection, a welcome counter balance to the discomfort caused by the sound the night before. The woman gave me another smile, this time with a little more sincerity as she saw my eyes light up.

"Go ahead in, see if any of them speak to you," she said, tilting her head in an encouraging manner toward the cat pit. I nodded and stepped over the meager barrier. The reaction was immediate. Every cat turned to me, eyes wide, and a chorus of hisses buffeted me like a rogue wave against the hull of a ship. I staggered backward, surprised and terrified and caught the heel of my shoe against the gate, bringing it down with me. The woman gave a shrill little squeal and tried to catch me as I went down, hard, on my bottom. The gate collapsed on top of me leaving nothing between the cats and the rest of the shelter. But they did not stampede out of their enclosure. The woman and I looked in bewilderment at the display of feline terror before us. Every single cat pressed their body up against the wall of cages opposite us and a low, gurgling hiss crept from their ranks. I righted myself as quickly as possible and reset the fence with the help of the woman. We looked at each other for a moment, her face an illustration of surprise and confusion. I stared back, barely quelled terror bubbling up in my gut.

I asked her, "Have you ever seen something like this?"

She turned her head back to the wall of cats and shrugged. "No. I mean, cats can be jumpy, but..." she paused. "Do...?" She looked back at me, clearly unsure of how to continue. "Do you still want one, or...?" She let the question hang, the answer seemingly so obvious I didn't feel the need to respond. Then she seemed to snap out of whatever spell had been cast and gave me a third smile, this one a little more wily. "Okay, you know what, I think you might have just moved to quickly and they got spooked is all. Hang on." She went back to the front desk, leaving me with the hum of feline distrust and fear. After a moment, I realized they were all staring at the same place: my prosthetic hand, dangling limp and useless to my left side. I put it behind my back and thought I saw the tension in their bodies' recede, if only a little.

The woman returned with a catnip mouse and handed it to me. "Try using this. It might do the trick."

I took the mouse from her and got down on my haunches, knees popping audibly as I descended. I reached over the fence and dangled the mouse, jerking its tail up and down and making uncertain cooing noises. I kept my stump firmly behind my back. Several of the cats watched the movement of the mouse as it twirled and pirouetted in the vaguely fetid air, others kept their gaze firmly on the spot just behind me. After a few moments, an orange and white tabby separated himself from the pack. He glanced back at his companions, then turned back to look at me. He didn't follow the motion of the twitching mouse, but instead locked his eyes on mine. The cat came forward, his paws testing every step; never looking at the mouse, only fixing his gaze on me. After a few steps, he broke my stare and turned his attention to the mouse. He trotted over and began batting at it, pulling it from my hand and rolling onto his back in pleasure. I watched him, still uncertain, then reached over and scratched the top of his head. He didn't seem to mind. I heard the woman sigh in relief behind me.

"Looks like Milo found a new home," she said. "I'll get the paper work." I brought him home in a carrying cage the woman provided free of charge. Milo played with the mouse all the way home.

When we arrived, I opened the door to his cage and Milo tumbled out, the mouse firmly between his teeth as he scampered into the kitchen, not sparing me a glance. I shut the front door and went to my armchair, crumpling into it. My body began to quiver slightly and I inhaled then exhaled deeply, trying to dispel the memory of what I'd just seen. That wall of cats. Their eyes riveted to my stump. I knew the image would make its way through my nightmares for the remainder of my life. Milo poked his head around the corner of the kitchen and mewled softly. The sound was lovely and I got up to fix him a plate of wet food.

That night, as expected, I dreamt of the cats. I stood in the shelter, gazing at the fenced off enclosure. The woman was nowhere to be seen and the lights in the room only gave off a dim and ghostly illumination. The same wall of fur and teeth and tails stood plastered to the wire of the cages as they stared at my stump. But they did not hiss. Their mouths were slightly open and a sound emanated from their maws, but not the low gurgling hiss I heard that afternoon. Instead, it was the low, pulsating thrum. It seemed to rock the cat's small bodies in time to its sinister rhythm and I watched them, a scream caught in my lungs. I felt bile simmering in my belly, and my head swam with nausea. The sound was far louder and more terrible than what I had heard before. It felt as if my body was being hit with a mallet from the inside, right at the center, metrically matching the horrific pulse in my ears. Then, out of the corner of my blurred vision, I saw Milo. He crept forward, ears flat as he stood in front of the others. His back arched, he gave a hiss from deep within his gut. His hiss was real; it was not whatever dreadful sound came from the throats of his comrades. He pulled back his body in a taught stance and gave a horrendous yowl, piercing through the deafening hum.

My eyes flew open and I could see only black. The thrum continued to palpitate and I could hear Milo yowl in agony and alarm. I felt coldness so deep and complete that my teeth began to chatter and my brain seemed to vibrate within the confines of my skull. I felt as if I was drowning in a frozen lake and I screamed, trying to catch my breath and repel the freezing air from my body. Milo's scream reached a new decibel and I sat up, vomiting into my lap, the hot stench rising to my nostrils and making me double over and retch again. I screamed, wishing for death and vomited once more.

And then it was over. The sound ceased and the cold left the room, leaving nothing but the stench of bile. Milo stopped screeching. I looked up and saw him silhouetted in the doorway, the light from the bathroom making him into the perfect shadow image. He cocked his head slightly and took a halting step into the room. He mewled, as if asking me what happened. I breathed in and out, air rushing over my burning vocal chords. I closed my eyes and began to cry, just silent tears at first, but they became full body sobs and I threw back my covers to escape the vomit and pulled my legs to my chest, heaving in great breaths of air. Something brushed against my arm and I flinched. I looked to my right and Milo was standing next to me, his tail twitching with fear, eyes wide. He cocked his head and mewled again and I pulled him to me, stroking him with my trembling good hand. He acquiesced and rested his body against mine. He did not purr.

The next morning I stripped the bed, threw the sheets in the wash and called Dr. Amleth's office. I had no idea if what happened to me was of medical significance, but I was too frightened not to seek help. I didn't think I could bear another incident like the night before. A few hours later, I sat in the small waiting room of Amleth's office. My knee bounced up and down as I stared at a small stain on the floor. A child played with a wire bead structure in the corner while her mother watched me warily. I glanced at her and she quickly looked back to the child. Self-consciously, I groped the small table next to me and pulled an issue of Better Homes & Gardens onto my lap. I opened to the middle of the magazine and reread the same sentence over and over until my name was called.

I followed the nurse back to Amleth's office, the phrase *Sphagnum, or peat moss, is a natural soil which is perfect for growing your roses* skipping through my head to the clip-clop rhythm of my halting gait. She opened the door, said my name to the doctor and motioned for me to step in. Amleth sat behind his desk, scribbling his signature over a stack of papers. He looked up and smiled when I came in, although I could tell he was not happy to see me. I extended my only hand and walked forward as I heard the door snap shut behind me. We shook and I sat down opposite him. With expectant eyes, he asked what the trouble was, his tone nervous. Putting the matter of my absent hand behind him had been difficult, I knew this. I also knew he was privately hoping that my visit had nothing to with it. I shifted, uncomfortable, in the wooden chair and, despite the anxiety I knew I would cause, told him about the events of the past couple days. As I gave him my story, sentences coming out faltering and disjointed, I began to hear how my story must have sounded to him. This was insanity that I was articulating. I was in the midst of describing the manic episode of a crazy person to Dr. Amleth, and I could see in his eyes he felt the same. I stumbled through the last bit of my story, how I vomited in my lap and how Milo gave me his small comfort, and I averted my gaze, feeling foolish and angry. I knew how he would respond.

For several moments, however, he didn't respond at all. I chanced a look at his face and didn't see the alarmed pity and anxiety expected, but instead a more understanding, gentle pity surprised me entirely.

"That sounds like hell, my friend," he said, true sympathy in his voice. "You've been through quite a lot lately and I'm sure this doesn't help with dealing with the loss of… uh… well…" he pointed vaguely at the air where my hand used to be. "And I know we haven't got a satisfying conclusion for what happened to you there. Who knows, I've seen things in my time that I couldn't even begin to explain with science or medicine. Often times, things occur that are just out of our realm of understanding, and nothing but time and years of study can do anything to further our knowledge." At this, he leaned back in his chair, and sighed, as if heaving off a great weight. "But what you experienced last night wasn't supernatural or cosmic or what have you. What you're describing sounds a lot to me like PTSD. It makes a considerable amount of sense if you think about it. The loss of your hand was a truly traumatic event. I'm sure it was utterly bewildering, especially since I, nor anyone else, could give you anything resembling a reasonable explanation. Hallucinations, unexplained physical maladies, confusion, night terrors; these are all symptoms of PTSD. And I'm glad you came to me. We don't have the tools to explain what happened to your hand, but we do have the tools to fight PTSD." He began talking about treatment options; therapy, medication, but I heard none of it. Something more pressing captured my attention.

I could feel my left hand again. I had experienced none of the phantom limb syndrome that had been so prevalent in all the literature given to me by Dr. Amleth. And besides the odd tingling when I had heard the noise, had not felt any pain or discomfort, not even the morning I found myself five fingers lighter. But now. Now I felt something. I stared down at my prosthetic hand, a sense of vertigo locking itself inside me as I sensed the impossible. Someone was holding my hand. And not in the casually romantic way lovers do as they walk down the street. Someone was holding my severed hand in their hands, turning it over, feeling the knuckles, pressing lightly against the flesh. But they weren't like any fingers I had felt against my skin before. For one thing, there were just too many. Instead of feelings eight fingers and two thumbs pressing and caressing my absent hand, I felt what must have been twenty fingers and many, many thumbs, feeling their way up and down my skin. I got the distinct impression what I was feeling was not many different people's hands stroking my palm and digits, but to many-fingered hands, moving in time and harmony, only in the way fingers attached to the same hand can. I could feel the length of the fingers, longer than a normal man's, and seemingly jointed in too many places. The skin on the alien hands was dry and rough and prickly, like the skin

106

of a kiwi. I recoiled my left arm in terror and disgust but the sensation followed. I shook it vigorously, panic beginning to rise in my chest. I became aware Dr. Amleth had stopped his monologue and was asking what was wrong, concern coloring his voice. Little sharp screams started to propel themselves from my mouth and I stood up, shaking my arm so forcefully the prosthetic came undone and thudded to the floor, revealing my smooth stump to the office. The many-fingered sensation grew more intense as the hands seemed to delight in the feeling of my abandoned flesh. It was too much. Black pounded at the edges of my vision and I saw Dr. Amleth come around his desk just as my eyesight blurred, then blackened as I toppled to the ground, unconscious.

I came to some hours later, lying in an unfamiliar bed with a bright light beating down on my clammy skin. A steady beep sounded in the corner. I opened my eyes and found myself in a hospital room. Pulling myself up so I was sitting fully upright, I glanced around the small room and spotted my prosthetic sitting in the chair next to my bed. I looked down at my stump. The sensation of the alien hands was gone and I had returned to the familiar lack of feeling where my hand used to be. I glanced at the clock on the wall. It was about 9:30 and I thought about Milo. He would be hungry by now.

Gingerly, I pulled the IV out of my arm and unclamped the pulse monitor from my finger. The machine stopped beeping and was replaced with a high-pitched drone. I attached my false hand and began searching the room for my clothes as a heavy-set nurse with a bored look on her face walked in.

"Sir, I need you to get back in bed, please," she said, standing in the doorway, arms crossed.

"Naw, naw," I said, my voice weak and dry. "I'm all better now. I need to get home and feed my cat."

"Your cat will be fine, sir, I need you to return to your bed. You had an episode and it's not safe for you to be walking around." A little pinch of fire ignited in my belly.

"I'm perfectly fine, where are my clothes?" I asked, pulling open the closet door. I saw my pants, shirt and shoes and pulled them down off the shelf.

"I'm afraid I can't do that until you've been fully examined, sir, I…"

"Look, lady," I said, turning to her, my voice no longer weak. "I need to get home to feed my fucking cat." I had begun pulling up my pants, doing the routine awkward jig that comes with dressing with only one hand. "So if you could just move aside and I'll sign whatever waiver you want me to or whatever-" I jerked my left pant leg upward and lost my balance, toppling onto my side and almost knocking the wind out of me. The nurse sighed and walked over, pulling me up by my handless left arm. I blushed, all the anger knocked out of me. "Is Dr. Amleth here?" I asked, my voice small again. She led me to the bed and pulled up my pants, zipping the zipper and buttoning the button with the expertise of someone who has done so many times. Gently, she pushed my chest so I was sitting on the bed and she did her best to smile at me.

"I'll go get him," she said. I mumbled a thank you and pulled the hospital gown off my torso. I pulled on my shirt and did my very best not to cry. Some level of adrenaline had been coursing through my veins for the last 48 hours and now that it had left, I was very, very tired. I just wanted to see Milo and fall asleep. Probably on my couch.

Dr. Amleth walked in followed by the nurse. His face was all concern and exhaustion and I realized I had put him through what was probably a very upsetting ordeal. A wave of guilt washed over me.

"Dr. Amleth, I'm sorry," I began, but he shushed me and shooed my legs up and back into the bed. He pulled out a stethoscope and started listening to my heart.

"Not at all, not at all. I won't be hearing any of that," he said, moving the cold steel over my bare chest. He listened for a few seconds, then pulled the tool away. He swung it around his neck and pulled out a penlight. His finger popped up and he moved it slowly back and forth. "Follow," he said. I did so, my pupils moving through the light, the image of my veins being thrown in and out of my vision. He clicked it off and crossed his arms. "How are you feeling?"

"Fine," I lied. "That was…" I thought of Milo. "I think you're right, Dr. Amleth. I experienced some, uh, phantom limb stuff back in your office." There was a large part of me that didn't believe it for a second, but I had to get out of this hospital as soon as possible. The way to do that wasn't through telling a doctor I thought some alien creature was somehow fondling my stolen hand. "Really, doc, I just need to sleep in my own bed tonight, I think." This was also a lie. I would be avoiding my room for a while.

Dr. Amleth regarded me silently for a few moments. He sighed threw his nose and gave a little half shrug.

"Alright," he said. "A familiar setting is probably best for you now. But we'll need to start treatment as soon as possible, okay?" I nodded, relatively certain I would be doing no such thing. "Okay," he said and began leading me out the door. At the door's precipice, he turned around and looked at me. "Except maybe… sleep on your couch tonight," he said, a wry, nervous smile on his face. I smiled back. At least we could agree on that.

I returned home to find Milo lying in my armchair, sleeping soundly. As the door clicked shut, his head perked up and he hopped off the chair and came to rub his body against my legs. I knelt down and stroked his back. Unthinking, I let my left arm sit on my thigh near his face and he gave a guttural little hiss and sauntered off into the kitchen. He looked around and tossed out a little mewl as he walked to his dish. I followed him and slipped in a puddle of liquid on the linoleum. I managed to right myself by grabbing the counter instead of clocking my head against the corner. What a charming little cherry that would be on the sundae that is my life. I looked down at the puddle and frowned. Grabbing some paper towels, I leaned down to wipe it up and recoiled as the stench of it hit my nose and realized it was Milo's urine. It was tangy and stung my eyes, far riper than any cat pee I'd smelled before. I looked at Milo, puzzled for a moment. But then I looked back at the puddle and paper towels and it clicked. That was the smell of Milo's fear pheromones. He had pissed himself out of fear. This must have been where he was when the sound started last night.

As if on cue, it returned. Suddenly and with wretched force, the low pulsing thrum filled my home and I clamped my hands over my ears. Milo gave his incendiary howl and I watched as a new puddle formed beneath him. He ran out of the kitchen and darted up the stairs, his screams reverberating behind him. Grabbing the paper towels, I wadded them into the tightest balls I could and stuffed one in each ear. It did not keep the infernal sound out, but it dampened it enough so that I could function.

This was far enough. I was not going to continue to live my life in fear and confusion, too scared to ever enter my bedroom again and sleep in my own sheets. I braced myself against the counter and took in several deep breaths, trying my best to calm my fluttering heart, which seemed to pulse in time to the hellish sound. I stood up, stepped over the urine and walked toward my bedroom.

The door stood slightly ajar and I could see the room inside was dark. The sound almost seemed to make physical ripples in the air as it oozed out the doorway. I walked slowly, stomach roiling and legs screaming in protest to go back, there was nothing this way but horror. I reached the door and pushed it inward, the dark creeping out and greeting me. The sound tumbled out and seemed to engulf me, to wrap its tendrils around me in a maniacal embrace. Little sobs escaped me in waves of fear and I reached my arm, my only arm with a hand, into the room and flipped on the switch.

There, right at my bedside, inches from where my head lay every night, was a ball of darkness. For a moment, my screaming mind could not discern what it looked at. It was a black sphere that rippled gently with each pulse of its terrible thrum as if it were the heart of the devil himself. It did not move. It was perfectly stationary, just centimeters above my nightstand. Except it wasn't. I looked closer and I realized that it was one, maybe two centimeters, submerged into my bedside table. I remembered staring at that exact place the day before, when I first heard the sound, knowing something was not quite right. Now I knew what it

110

was; the left side of my night table had been slightly, just slightly lower than the right. The answer clicked in my brain with such force that I cried out and toppled to the floor, staring at the horrible, black orb.

I knew what happened to my hand. My sleeping position never varies. I cannot fall asleep unless I'm on my right side, my right arm curled against my body, and my left arm draped over the side of the bed. Draped so my hand would dangle in the exact place where I now beheld the lightly pulsing orb. It took the shards of my nightstand. And then it took my hand. I was staring at a portal. Some rip in the time-space continuum. Some terrible door to some alien world where the creatures had many fingers and loved the way my flesh felt on their skin. Gulping air, trying to steady myself, I slowly rose to my feet. There was a part of myself that was very calmly telling me the only thing between utter insanity and walking away from this relatively intact was the little bits of paper towel lodged deep in my ears. I pushed the bits of paper deeper and took a step into my room.

The thrumming grew more intense with every step. I moved closer and closer and finally, at about six feet from the orb, I could move no further. Every molecule of my body vibrated in protest and said *No. No Further.* I obeyed the command, as I was unsure what would transpire after that next step. The blackness of it was beautiful. Unbearably, undeniably beautiful. I was certain this was what scientists meant when talking about black holes. No light could escape this yawning chasm of darkness. As the portal's beat throbbed through me, I could feel my grip on sanity growing tenuous and knew there was only so much time I could spend in this room before my mind snapped and I hurled myself at the thing, legs akimbo, cackling in anticipation for what awaited me on the other side. The idea was already attractive and I had to will my eyes to look away, to find something to distract me from infinity. They lingered, with all the petulant whining of a child wanting to stay for one more ride at the amusement park and I had to slap my hand over them and jerk my head away, forcing my eyes off the exquisite prize that was the privilege to gaze upon the infinite.

THE ABSCENT HAND

When I removed my hand, my eyes snapped open and landed upon one of my slippers. Old, ragged, bitten by long lost canine companions, it sat dejected in the corner of my room. An idea blossomed and spun about in my delicate mind and I lurched toward it, my goal resolute and teetering on the edge of sanity. I picked it up with a feverish lunge and turned back toward the vibrating black heart of Satan. With magnificent anticipation, I hurled the slipper toward the portal and watched it abandon momentum once it hit the inky black, sending dramatic ripples through the orb, and slowly sinking into the abyss, making liquid gurgles as it went. As the heel disappeared, a sound like a pebble hitting a pond sprang from the portal, but deeper and somehow with the air of sentience. As if it burped after a good meal. I continued to gaze at the place where my slipper vanished and I could feel the desire to surrender myself pulling at my innards. A harsh, base yearning that took every ounce of my sane self to fight against, screaming that that way only lies death.

But then, something happened. The orb began to change shape. Something protruded out of the gloom. A thick film of the blackness seemed to strain against what was coming through, and then it burst, leaving a hole, which something was now coming through. As I watched, I realized it was my slipper, coming toe first. With what appeared to be great effort, the slipper came inch by inch, quivering with exertion as it came back to my world, the world in which it belonged. But after about half of it had come through, I realized that it was not entering of its own volition. Wrapped around the midsection of the slipper, was a hand. Its hue a deep bluish-green, with thick, short bristles sprouting from every pore. Each finger had too many joints. And there were many, many fingers.

As the hand intruded, slipper in its grasp, the deep pulsating rhythm from the portal was matched by a high-pitched sound that beat in time with its lower count point. They rang together in a deafening, bone rattling harmony that sounded like the trumpet of Gabriel, come to reclaim the Earth. I dropped to my knees and let silent tears pour down my face. I could feel myself splintering apart as I beheld this being, reaching across space and time, gouging itself through a hole in the very fabric of reality, all to return my slipper. The harmony reached a fever pitch of such ecstatic, euphonious cacophony I could feel the boards below my knees begin to give way and the house shake with the burden of its note. I watched the hand push forward until it was just below a scaly wrist. And then a sound, delicate and swift, a sound that could not be discerned from a soap bubble popping next to your ear, and the orb was gone.

The thud of the severed hand hitting the floor was so mundane, so usual, that I was certain my mind had decided to vacate the premises and leave me with the pleasing image of my bedroom without the hole in space encroaching upon my nightstand. I did not look at the hand right away, but rather gaped at the spot where just a moment before the infinite had chosen to open its empty eye. But after some time, my own eyes drifted down to where the alien hand now laid, my slipper still clutched in its scabby grasp. I rose, slowly, and with the feeling of wandering through a dream, I approached the hand. It was wider than I thought. It had at least two-dozen fingers, and four thumbs on either side. With all the thoughtfulness of a child reaching for an unknown animal at its feet, I poked the skin just above the wrist. It gave slightly and from just the pad of my finger, I could feel the foreignness of the viscera beneath. And I knew- somewhere, in some unimagined place, there was a creature feeling my poke in the space its hand used to be. A low growl came from behind me.

I looked around and there was Milo, staring at the hand, every hair on his back standing at attention. I gave the hand one last look, and then turned on my heels, scooped up Milo before he knew what I was doing and bolted out the front door, grabbing my keys as I left. Dropping Milo in the passenger seat, I slid in and turned the key in the ignition. As the car roared to life, I looked out the window back at my house. It looked the same as it ever had. Someday, someone would come to check on me and they would find it empty. A realtor would find the severed hand and pass it off as some novelty the previous, clearly unstable owner left behind. But they would not be able to deny the uncanny sensation holding the thing in their hands would bring. They would not be able to deny the sensation of horrid connection brought by touching the weird, bristly thing. I did one glance around the block. Several lights had turned one, undoubtedly to investigate the source of that unusual, disturbing sound that had woken them from their sleep. Perhaps there would be someone to check up on me sooner than I thought. Then I wondered if the next time the blackness swallowed up the space just above my nightstand, would there be someone in the house to witness? Would they be there when the owner of the hand tried to climb back through to reclaim what it had lost?

At this thought, I dropped my foot to the gas, throwing Milo against the fabric of the seat, yowling in protest. I did not look back. Instead, I looked down at the stump resting against the steering wheel where my hand used to be. And I prayed to whatever God there was I would die before I ever saw that yawning black chasm again. I drove deeper into the blackness, hoping there was someone listening.

Colin grew up in the small, rural town of Putney, Vermont at the edge of what were probably haunted woods. He has had nightmares since he was little and to this day is afraid of his closet. He suffers from crippling night terrors that he uses as fuel for stories.

Colin attended Bennington College where he studied Acting, Video Production and Literature. His only publication history is with his alma mater's literary magazine, The Silo. He hikes dogs through New Jersey by day and acts and writes by night. He currently resides in Brooklyn, NY with a closet full of demons.

Beyond the Dead

Brian D. Mazur

Anyone would have stopped at the sight of a giant creature with long hair and twisted limbs; Sam Hunt did because he was a photographer. What made the scene perfect for him was the man dressed in gray who stood in the foreground behaving as if fighting off something unseen with flailing arms.

"*Torment Juxtaposed*", he would name the photograph.

The paved road doglegged left and a worn path made by a tractor lay in front of him. He followed the road to the left, pulled his old 1983 Challenger over onto the shoulder, stones crunching under the tires.

Sam jumped out of the car, his camera in hand. Hanging the strap over his shoulder, he walked on the grass alongside the tractor path. To his left stood a worn house with a wraparound porch and a barn a few hundred yards away, the land surrounded by the remnants of long dead vegetation. A forest of barren trees ran twenty feet back along the other side of the dirt road into the distance beyond. The creature at the top of the path was an old, dead tree, the trunk grown like twists of ropes, covered in moss and brown vines that reached to the ground, the roots like a rotting skirt.

Heavy clouds covered the November sky. The chilly air smelled of musty earth and burnt wood.

Sam turned to the man standing on the path, snapping a picture. He loved black and white photography. The late afternoon, gloomy cloud cover, and the man dressed in gray, would make a perfect shot. He clicked off two more pictures from different angles.

Sam studied them in the view screen, and then turned his attention back to the man.

"Hey, do you mind if I get a closer shot of you?" Sam shouted holding his camera up, hoping the gesture would indicate he was a professional photographer.

There was no response, just the sound of crows in the distance and leaves ticking across the hardpan road. The man faced Sam, but Sam had the feeling he looked beyond him. He glanced back to where he thought the gray man stared. The view on the other side of the paved road was the same as where he stood; the dirt road continued across a field to woods in the distance.

Turning back, the man waved his hands in front of himself, as if wiping something away. He walked backward, still facing Sam, still waving. Then he stumbled back as if he no longer controlled his body.

Sam raised his camera and snapped off a few more shots. The further the gray man fell away, the more he seemed to blend in with the fall surroundings. Sam followed him, continuously pressing the shutter release.

When the gray man reached the tree, he disappeared.

Sam lowered the camera. Did the man walk around the tree? How would he have missed that?

"Can I help you?"

Sam jumped at the sudden voice. An old man, tall and thin, waited patiently for Sam to answer, puffing on a cigarette.

"Geez, man, you scared the hell out of me," Sam gasped.

The old man continued smoking his cigarette. His skin, tanned and leathery, hung loose about the throat; the eyes, overshadowed by bushy brows and a large hooknose, appeared small, like a bird's. He was dressed in a smudged blue shirt and gray pants with cigarette burn holes. An old green baseball cap sat crooked on his head.

"I'm sorry," Sam said. "I usually don't just step onto someone's property without talking to them first." He held up his camera. "I saw that dead, old tree and a man standing on this path. I thought it was a great opportunity."

The old man continued staring at him.

"And you don't care," Sam finished.

The old man dropped the remainder of his cigarette and ground it into the earth with an old work boot. He looked up and down the road.

"Don't see no man," he rasped.

What remained of the old man's teeth were crooked and tobacco stained stumps.

"Look," Sam offered, showing him the pictures in his camera.

The old man shook his head without looking.

Sam continued, "He acted strange. Just staring into nothing, and waving his arms around like swatting flies."

"Did he now?" He paused a moment, looking Sam in the eyes. "The name's Sanders," he said, extending a hand.

Sam hesitated in surprise, before reaching out to shake Sander's hand. It felt like tree bark.

"Sam Hunt. I'm planning to put a book together. I've been driving all over the country."

"Have yah now?"

"That tree," Sam said, "it's a great picture opportunity, but it looks kind of out of place with the rest of your land."

Sanders stared at the tree with a blunt gaze. "It's necessary," he said.

"Necessary? How so?"

Sanders looked to Sam, "You hungry?" he asked, avoiding the question. "I've got a pot of chicken stew on the stove; fresh chicken, potatoes, carrots, and just the right seasoning. The missus left me the recipe. I've got plenty."

Sam considered the abrupt invitation from the odd stranger. All this time on the road, he'd been cautious selecting which personal invitation to accept. However, the meal did sound better than fast food. As for Sanders . . . Sam slid a hand into a pants pockets, right hand wrapping around his trusty Smith & Wesson pocketknife, finding assurance in the cold metal.

Standing there, he could smell the dinner now and his stomach growled at the mere mention of it. He thought about it, he hadn't eaten since noon.

"That sounds great, Sanders. I appreciate it," he said, giving the knife one last squeeze.

"Bring your car up close to the house. See yah at my kitchen table."

Inside the house, Sam noticed piles of magazines, newspapers around the living room. It not only looked clean, but smelled that just cleaned freshness only lemony chemicals could give it, making it even feel clean. The furniture had no dust, area rugs no lint or dirt, and the polished wood floors allowed the minimal light to reflect from the sconces on the walls.

The kitchen itself was void of stacks of dirty dishes, bowls, and unfinished food. It was, in fact, immaculate. The stew boiled on the stove; bubbling as steam dispersed the stomach-growling aroma around the room.

"The missus always said that the kitchen should be the cleanest room in the house. It not only inspires fine food, but is welcoming to guests."

Sam nodded in agreement.

"Have a seat," Sanders offered, sliding an old tan mug of coffee across the white kitchen table, then turned to the stove where he ladled soup into bowls.

For a few moments, both men ate in silence. The stew was the most delicious Sam ever tasted. The flavors danced on his taste buds and sated his hunger.

"You mentioned a wife," Sam said, between spoonfuls.

Sanders nodded and shoveled more stew into his mouth.

Sam waited, taking a swallow of coffee, which also was the best he'd ever had.

"Yup," Sanders said, staring intently into his bowl. "Claire – she's been gone some time now."

"Sorry to hear that."

Sanders waved a hand. "No need. That's life, ain't it? Just like two daughters moving on." He glanced at Sam, before taking another spoonful. "What about you? You gotta a wife or girl?"

The old man's gaze burned through him, analyzing the short, curly hair, thin form, and Buddy Holly style glasses. He no doubt figured a geek like him would never get a girl; most people assumed the same.

Sanders put his mug down. "Sorry, I'm getting personal. Claire always called me a romantic. I enjoy hearing happy endings."

Sam shrugged. "No romantic stories here."

Sanders nodded. "Too busy with your book; I understand. Youth is the time to live life unfettered. Do what you want, when you want ... enjoy the spring of your life."

"Something like that."

The men continued to eat, each spoonful now accompanied by small talk. By the time they were done, Sam realized it was dark. Glancing at his watch, he realized it was after eight. Where did the time go?

As if reading his mind, Sanders offered Sam a bed for the night.

"It ain't fancy, but the sheets are clean and the bed is a queen; plenty of room to spread out. Tomorrow is going to be a sunny day, not too many of those this time of year. Get up early enough you can get some worthwhile shots at sunrise."

Sam felt the comfort of the folded knife press into his thigh. Then he considered a home cooked meal, an offer of a bed to sleep in... with a smile Sam didn't hesitate to accept the generous offer.

It seemed an impulsive stop turned out to be a lucky night.

The tree bled from the ropey trunk and twisted branches, dripping from the vines to curling leaves that looked like gnarled fingers, pooling over the roots. The dark fluid ran through the dead blades of grass around the base of the trunk, pouring into a giant open maw at the roots where rows of thin nail-like teeth shone, drinking in the former life giving fluid.

Voices came from the inky depths beyond the teeth, rising in the form of vapor. The mumblings were hard to understand. Sam leaned into the sounds, the inky depths, smelling of earth and old blood.

Sam felt a touch to his back, as he pitched forward down the hole.

He awoke with a start. Lying on his right side, he stared into the endless dark, heart hammering in his chest as he ran a hand through sweaty hair. The sheets were clean, but didn't cover the musty odor of the soft mattress and it irritated his nose and eyes.

Then, like an animal sensing a threat, his ears drew to attention.

He was not alone.

The air chilled him as if it had been in his dream. He blinked, hoping the action would make the dark less dense and quelled his fear.

It didn't work.

Come on, Sam, the dream's playing with your head.

Rolling over, he recognized the smell of earth and bad meat.

He turned his head to the left.

There, glowing out of the darkness from the other side of the bed was a woman, her head resting on a bloodstained pillow. Her face white with death, and splattered with blood; the eyes wide with terror, and the mouth opened in a silent scream, showed dry lips, and teeth broken and stained red.

Sam scrambled back, falling out of bed, banging his elbow on the floor, forcing the grip on his knife to loosen; it dropped away into the tangle of the bedding. The pain in the elbow assured him he was awake.

Kicking and flailing, he desperately freed himself from the sheets and then staggered across the room.

The woman, hair a wild tangled mess, sat up, raising her right arm, pointing an accusatory pale finger in his direction. Her mouth remained mutely open.

Sam stumbled to the bedroom door and out into the endless black of the hall. It was an unnatural darkness. Total and complete. Reaching out, his fingers brushed the wall next to him, his hip running into a table, followed with the sharp sound of something shattering on the floor.

From which direction had he come up here? He couldn't remember. Continuing his way down the hall, he felt the ridges and tears of old wallpaper under his fingers, and occasionally, the frame and smooth glass of a picture.

His fingers brushed a doorframe. Rubbing his hand along the panels of the door, he searched for the knob, and found it. He tried twisting it left and right, but it wouldn't open.

"Damn."

Moving his way down the hall, he bumped into another table. Newspapers and magazines slid to the floor. A couple more steps and he slipped on what fell, rolling him over onto his back.

Unhurt, Sam lunged back onto his feet.

He wasn't sure which direction he'd been moving.

The dark wrapped itself around him, feeling cool and clammy.

"Sanders!" he screamed.

An invisible finger drew a cold line down his spine. He no longer felt alone.

"Sanders, that you?"

He moved again, keeping hands on the old wallpaper.

"Sanders!" he screamed again.

Then – a wall in front of him

Having chosen the direction, Sam had reached the end of the hall.

"Shit!" he whispered, slapping the plaster.

A strumming pulsed in his ears as the dark seemed to undulate.

It's coming...

...coming...

...coming...

A white figure emerged in front of him. Shadows peeled away from her scarred face and tattered clothes. Deep cuts in her cheeks, forehead, and chin; mouth open in a silent roar. It was an older woman with wild salted hair, arms extended, hands curled into talons, and eyes fevered with death.

With a cry, Sam twisted out of the way, his back hitting the wall behind him. Eyes wide, he watched as the ghostly figure melted into the dark. He hesitated a moment, taking comfort in the solidity of the wall;

121

the realness of it gave him a moment to gather himself.

Cautiously he moved toward his room, pausing in front of the doorway. A sliver of light shone through the slightly open door. It creaked open further, as if offering entrance. He made out half the bed, blankets partially on the floor where he had fallen off; behind that stood the night side table. Though he didn't see her, the white haired woman could be in hiding in the shadows. Problem was all his belongings were in there and he didn't want to stay in this hell any longer.

At once, shrieks reverberated from the dark, one over the other, over the other. Separate voices, screamed in terror and agony. Raspy, cold cries begged for mercy and received none as the roars escalated.

In a panic, Sam burst through the door of the bedroom, without concern for what had been on the other side. He grabbed his duffle bag at the foot of the bed; the screams pushing him. From the bedside table he swept up the car keys. Tossing the sheets and blankets aside, he dug out his shoes and found the pocketknife.

Leaving the room, Sam headed toward the stairs that lay ahead to his left.

The shrieks stopped.

The ensuing silence was just as deafening, maybe more so.

The stairway yawned open at his feet. The darker shadows at the foot of the stairs seemed to eat their way up, step-by-step. He had to get out, despite his fear to move. Sam proceeded down, slow and soft, the further he descended the more the dark gave way.

On the bottom floor, through an amber light in the living room, stood a man with his back to Sam. His hair was grey and he wore blue flannel pajamas. Over his shoulder, he saw the man reading a book.

"Sanders," he called.

The man continued to read, ignoring him. .

Sam glanced at the front door to his left; then broke for it.

Locked.

There was no dead bolt or latch lock. The knob would not turn.

Dropping everything but the knife, Sam stormed back to the living room. He clicked open the serrated knife blade.

"Sanders!" Sam screamed. "Look at me, Sanders! Damn it, I want out – I want out now! This place is fu…"

The book dropped out of Sanders' hands, hitting the wood floor with a loud slap, pages opened face up. Arms dangling loosely by his sides, Sanders stood unmoving, staring straight at the wall in front of him.

"Sanders, what the hell are you doing? Do you hear me? Let me out of this hell hole," Sam demanded.

Then Sanders spun as if on a pivoting platform.

Only this was not Sanders.

The man had the same slender build, but a receding hairline, a wider nose, fuller lips, and large hands. He stood facing Sam, eyes staring dully at him. Then, he leaned his head back, throat ripped open. A jagged slice from one ear to the other yawned horrifically open. His larynx, shredded, hung in strands like raw meat.

Blood flowed, covering the man's chest in a dark red bib and spread down the front of his blue pajamas to the floor around his feet. As it ran in the wood grain, it looked like blood flowing through veins. A gurgling sound emanated from the torn throat, as if trying to speak. He raised a blood-covered hand, pointing a dripping finger toward Sam.

The blood gathered on the floor, then rushed toward Sam like a pool of water pouring from a forgotten left-on garden hose. The knife slipped from his grasp and fell into the blood. Breathlessly he stumbled down the hall toward the kitchen. The stench of blood filled the air. His stomach churned; he bent over and vomited.

Hands shaking, he wiped his mouth with the back of his hand.

When he turned back around, he saw the blood gone.

All Sam could hear or feel was the thunderous hammering of his heart.

"Sanders!" he screamed, hands balled into fists, vocal chords strained from the energy he put into his rage. "Sanders!"

The blood tang, replaced by the chicken stew from last night that now smelled less appetizing.

He made his way through the kitchen and to the back door.

The knob didn't move either.

"San... Sanders. P-Please... l-let me out," he said, his voice a soft whisper.

He slapped the door; leaving his hand there, resting his forehead on the back of it, eyes closed. Breathing heavily, sweat dripped into his eyes and off his nose. He curled and uncurled his hand on the door, like a cat sharpening its claws; the friction burned his fingertips

Then there came whistling. It was a low, tuneless sound, coming from a distance.

Sam lifted his head.

The sound drifted about the house; fading in and out.

Then, *Yellow Submarine* whistled into his ear.

Sam gasped and spun around.

He was still alone.

Yellow Submarine continued to glide around the room. It came from all directions.

Collapsing, Sam clasped his hands over his ears, folding over until his head touched the floor. It was this position that cut his senses off, made him unaware of the world around him, something he didn't realize as a blow to his head turned his world black.

Sam woke to the rising sun peeking through the distant trees. The murky silhouette of Sanders squatted in front of him, twirling Sam's knife in his hands. He wore the same clothes as the night before, along with the familiar baseball cap. Beside him, a round point shovel lay on the ground, covered in old dirt and blood; the thing that knocked Sam cold, he figured. Next to that was Sam's Canon.

"*Yellow Submarine*, it was my daughters' favorite song when they were little. It has that nursery rhyme sound to it, don't you think?" Sanders said, as he spun the folded knife between both his index fingers. "That's why I whistled it when I killed them... even as teenagers I figured it would still put them at ease, allowing me to come up on them without raising suspicion." He clicked the blade open and made a slashing motion in front of himself, the point fixed on Sam. "That didn't go quite as planned."

Sam lay on the ground, stones digging into his back, his head throbbing. He climbed back to his feet. Sanders rose with him. Looking about, he gradually realized he was on the same tractor path where he saw the gray man yesterday.

"Sitting in the backyard that evening, drinking too much, I thought a bit about the farm not doing so well. The summer had been hot and dry, just like the previous two. Damage to the crops cut off our money supply, our ability to survive. I guess I felt bad about the situation I put us. The more I drank, the more a voice whispered in my head. It was kind of pleasant, so I kept tipping back ol' Jack, enjoying the 'company'." Sanders shook his hand next to his right ear. "Before I knew it, that voice rattled my brain. I found my thoughts not my own. It said if I took care of Claire, it would stop talking to me. I knew what it meant by that. She was asleep when I entered our bedroom that night. Pressed a pillow to her face and then..."

Sanders made an up and down motion with Sam's knife.

"She put up a tussle, but didn't make a sound. Afterward, when things calmed down, I thought about what I'd done and how it would affect my daughters. I couldn't stand the thought of my girls living without their mom, so"-he shrugged-"Susan, my youngest, woke up when I entered with that knife raised over my head. My whistling didn't drown out her screams. Kate ran in, saw, and she started screaming." Sanders looked back to the house. "I got her in the kitchen. Then the voices just stopped. The silence after - the coldest thing I've ever heard."

In the rays of the rising sun, Sam thought he saw a bloody hole in the back of the old man's skull. He raised his arm to block the rays for a better look. Sanders turned back, looking at him with those cold, soulless eyes.

"All I was left with was the guilt; took care of that though." Using his hand like a pistol, he pointed two fingers into his mouth, flicking his thumb like a trigger.

Sam stepped back. "W-why you telling me this?" he asked.

A smile curled Sanders lips; a smile that didn't reach his eyes.

"You and me... we're the same."

Sam said in a tight voice, "I'm nothing like you."

The cold smile returned to Sanders mouth, his lips now cracked and peeling. "Oh, you're right about that. The difference between you and me and all the others that come here is numbers."

"Num...?"

"You've killed so many haven't you Sam Hunt? Far more than my three; just with this little old knife," Sanders said, pointing the blade at Sam. Then he bent down and picked up the camera. "Nice cover you had, using this thing. Take a few friendly shots, some friendly conversation, get them to relax with you, and then they were yours, isn't that right?"

Sam didn't respond.

"Doesn't matter how, or your motivations," Sanders continued, shrugging. "Indifferent mother to her abusive boyfriend; abusive father maybe, or maybe you just wanted to know what it felt like to kill somebody, to watch the life drain out of them and found you liked it. Don't matter, really. I'll also bet you've lost track of how many you've..." Sanders slashed the knife back and forth in front of him, laughing.

Sam found his legs and started to move. "I'm getting out of here."

"No, you're not."

Sam tried to step off the old road; it immediately felt like he'd walked into a wall. Looking down he saw his dirty stained gray pants and too large gray shirt. His memory flashed to the gray man.

No, he wasn't going anywhere.

"You've got some visitors coming, young man. They're on their way." He nodded down the road. "They'll be here soon."

"Where am I?" Sam asked, though knowing the answer.

"This is Between... a sort of weigh station. You're on the road to hell, boy." Sanders nodded to the tree. "They'll be taking you there, one of the gates to hell. That it's purpose I mentioned. "

Panic grew in Sam's stomach.

"Did you know this is my hell?" Sanders asked. "My hell is to stay here for all eternity to babysit every serial killer who comes by." He leaned in closer to Sam, but was careful not to break the plane between the two worlds. "Every night I also have to relive what brought me here. Those screams you heard, them were my girls as I slashed them"

"Th-those people I saw?"

"Oh, they were some of your victims. Don't you remember them?"

Sam dropped to his knees, covering his head with hands and arms. Now he did. He remembered them, and more.

"Oh, God," he cried.

"Too late for God," Sanders said. "Tick-tock, Sam."

Sam looked up to see dozens moving up the path as if they were floating. At that moment, the sun finished rising over the trees, flooding the group in golden sunshine, as if God were guiding their way.

They reached the blacktop, and then as if he had taken a picture, *snap*, they were on his side of the worn road. Men and women with skin of white and clothes of black, moved in determined fashion toward him. No children though. Only sick, insane people would harm a child. Monsters, things in human faces, yet they were far from being human.

Sam backed away, stumbling as the group drew closer. Like another snapshot taken with his camera, they wore faces twisted in hatred.

Snap! They drew closer.

Snap! Open jagged slashes to the faces and torsos.

Snap! Oozing stab wounds.

Snap! Throats ripped open and giant stains of blood turned black, smeared on their clothing.

They moved with disturbing silence.

"They're here to escort you into eternity."

Sam continued moving back, panting.

Before he knew it, they were around him, grabbing him about the arms and chest hauling him down the path. As each hand clutched at him it was as if an electrical shock shook his body. In his head, he saw what he had done to each of them, blood, screams, and artistic violence.

Each remembrance brought a new jolt and it all seemed endless.

He twisted and fought, but to no avail. He wanted to scream, not because it would do him any good, but because he had to, he needed to vocalize his angst, but a hand clamped around this throat and squeezed off any sound he could make.

They didn't look down at him, instead their gazes focused on the dead tree. He couldn't see the tree, but could smell it - the stench of wet, rotting wood and decomposing bodies.

Above, spindly branches of the tree loomed and hung between the heads and faces of his escorts like snakes; the strands brushed against their faces, unnoticed. The group turned him around, passing him from hand to hand, until he faced the ropey trunk of hell's gate.

They held him above a gaping hole at the base of the tree; moans and faint screams emanated up with the vapor that rose from the orifice, damp, and reeking. Sam looked down into the black where a pair of pale arms, stained with dirt and blood, reached through the darkness, fingers tipped with shiny, black curled talons. The fingers writhed with hunger.

The group tilted Sam downward.

The hand holding his throat slipped away and Sam began to scream. The sound didn't project past his mouth. At that moment, he recalled what he told all his victims, *"Go ahead, and scream. Scream as loud as you want. No one will hear you."* Then he would stop their screams, with a slash, and gushing blood.

He laughed at the irony of his situation.

Then all hands released him.

He fell into the talons that tore into his neck, ripped his arms, and bore in his chest. The arms pulled him down into the swirling darkness, the stench of death and the cinders of hell surrounded him, ushering Sam into his new home.

With publishing credits *including Raven and the Darkness, What She Dreams, Home Coming, Oh, Dark Tumbleweed, Shattering Glass, Dumaine,* and *Simple,* Brian Mazur is no stranger to having his name in print. The last twenty years have seen numerous publications in smaller press magazines as well, including *House of Pain, Outer Darkness, Graveworm Press, MindMares,* and *Mythic Circle.*

Peepers

Bruce Harris

Rachel married a skinhead. Dude's a vile, angry, self-absorbed, ignorant, and hateful waste of a life. Me? This isn't about me. "Live with it," my wife said. "Your daughter's an adult capable of making her own decisions. It's her life, not yours or mine. If he makes her happy and he's good to her that's all we need to know." She reminds me daily this isn't about me. So, I live with it, like walking around with a fucking catheter stuck up my pecker day and night.

"How high is the sky?" an easier question to answer then to figure out why nice women go for guys like James Jennings. I see stories about them all the time in the newspapers and read online and watch on the televised news. Some dumb wit falls for a scumbag doing life for first-degree murder. Another gets stuck on some son of a bitch who robs her blind until nearly penniless, yet, there she is, defending the jackass who destroyed her life. Humans do a lot of strange things.

The first time I laid eyes on Jennings caused permanent brain scar tissue. He gazed down at the gold Star of David around my neck. His smile disappeared faster than a Sandy Koufax fastball. Hell, it didn't take an Einstein to see my jewelry upset him. I'm sure he thought to himself that he recovered nicely, that I hadn't noticed his unbridled contempt, but he was wrong. A fucking bigot's eyes give him away every time. He acted like a gentleman in the presence of my wife and me, but his Eddie Haskell routine was as transparent as a school of glass catfish.

Where did it all go wrong? If you ask my wife, things are just honky dory, but blind eyes aren't where I come from. We raised our daughter to respect authority, other people, love thy neighbor, and blah blah blah. She was Bat Mitzvah at aged 13 like all of the other kids in the neighborhood. I look back at the photos, the wonderment in her expression, curiosity, her hunger to explore and learn, now satiated by a subhuman. Not that I, or we, are super religious or anything like that, but we believe in a supreme being. I had always envisioned a nice, clean-cut man for my daughter. A multi-tattooed, pierced, shaved-headed hater of humanity, someone who blamed everyone and everything else other than his own shortcomings, wasn't part of the equation. Neither was a motherfucker, who along with his ignorant buddies, defiled cemeteries. Jewish, Christian, it didn't matter to these cretins. Hell, it was all shits and giggles for them. Rachel deserved so much better than Jennings. But, who was I to stand in the way of her happiness?

It should have been the most memorable day of our lives, the day I walked down the aisle to give my daughter's hand away in marriage. One we'd all celebrate together for who the hell knew how long. What's more gratifying in life than the marriage of your only child? My camera had documented her life, from pre-school to nursery school to Girl Scouts to high school, and beyond. Whack! It might as well have been a Mike Tyson fist to the puss. Rachel, studying for her Ph.D. in Clinical Psychology at an Ivy League University, her limitless potential stretched before her like a North Dakota highway, waylaid by scum of the earth, a piece of shit, a hopeless hater, loser, and malcontent christened James Jennings.

It was one of those cold, clammy nights when darkness descended too early. A week prior, the clocks were turned back one hour and my body still hadn't adjusted to the changing season. The calendar read November. The 9th of November to be exact. Fucking day. Kristallnacht, known as the Night of Broken Glass, when Nazis destroyed Jewish buildings with sledgehammers, leaving the streets covered in pieces of smashed windows. Now reduced to a remembrance. An occurrence not to be forgotten, the calendar date ensures that each year. It stares you in the eyes and seizes you by the throat and it shakes you from your protected bearings.

The vodka bottle drained, I drank the remains of half a bottle of Slivovitz and stared at the creased black and white photo of my grandparents, smiling in front of their butcher shop in the center of a small village in what my mother always called "the old country." Short, holding hands, smiling, they were in another place, in another time, in November 1938 as it turns out, less than 24 hours before their glass houses and teeth shattered, the smiling, and their lives abruptly stopped. The warmth of the alcohol relaxed me. It always did. I thought about Rachel, always do. That gave me the will to continue another day, week, month, and year. I shut my eyes and dreamed. I dreamed the dream, again. It provided comfort, serenity. During nightly prayers, I'd ask for the dream. Not sure what a shrink would say about that, but I'm not losing any sleep over it.

I drove the Panzer II tank over his beautifully manicured sod and through the curved bay front window. House lights automatically illuminated. Steering wasn't easy, but I managed to maneuver the big tank up the staircase, obliterating everything, crushing the feebly locked bedroom door. His shocked expression is always the same when the big tank storms into his room, coming to a stop at his bed. I take in the swastika art and Hitler photos staining the walls, and drag him by the pajama shirt to the center of the room. I would have preferred to grab him by the hair, but the son-of-a-bitch's shaved head prevented that. He looked at me with a vacuous, expression, balling up his fists, ready to strike.

Earwax and blood covered the Q-tip. Mostly blood. "You'll need to listen more carefully, Jimmy Boy, because what I am about to do to your eyes will, how should I put this, render them superfluous. You do know the meaning of the word?" The poor bastard had a quizzical look on his face. "Read my lips. In about two minutes, your eyes will be removed from their sockets. Get it? So, I want to make certain your ears are nice and clean because without the ability to see, you'll be relying on your ears more than ever." He tried speaking, but only an indistinguishable high-pitched animalistic sound spilled forth from his voice box. That was just as well. My priority at that moment was not to be a good listener. I bunched a couple of the used Q-tips together and swabbed the waxy-bloody ends of the stained cotton underneath his nose and painted a yellowish-dark red Hitler-like moustache. I took a step back and admired my work. "There now, you look so much like that photo of the monster over your bed. Now you're ready to celebrate your special holiday in style!"

None of the cemetery desecraters received jail time. The judge took their age into consideration when sentencing Jennings and his three hoodlum friends and pronounced a too lenient sentence, one in which the four punks received probation and community service. During sentencing, the judge pointed out her decision was partly based on the fact the boys had showed contrition during the trial and she felt the probation coupled with a mandatory education class about the Holocaust was fair and appropriate. Fuck that. But, as it turned out, the judge was seventy five percent correct.

My boot was on his throat. "Now, Jennings, now that your ears have been cleaned, can you hear me loud and clear?" He didn't respond. The dopey look on his face bored me. "Let me remind you that not too long ago, the artist in you decided to spray paint obscene and offensive symbols and slurs at the Green Hill Cemetery. I know it was just a case of boys being boys. Right? Well, you know what, the judge cut you a break, gave you a chance I wouldn't have given you. Your three buddies seemed to have straightened themselves out and are now leading very productive lives. All three of them in fact said that the Holocaust class they had taken had opened their eyes, but not you!" For some reason, I found that humorous.

Speaking to reporters from his hospital bed, a badly bruised boy recounted his ordeal. A large bandage covered the top of his head and upper half of his face, down to his nostrils. I clicked the television remote to turn up the sound because it was difficult to understand the poor guy as he strained to speak through a broken jaw. He explained to the reporter that he was a Hassidic Jew, and went on to describe the beating he endured two weeks prior. The victim had just come from a homeless kitchen where he regularly volunteered his time after school helping to feed the hungry and homeless, when he was jumped from behind, beaten unmercifully, and left for dead. The helpless victim didn't get a look at his assailant, but he remembered hearing racial slurs throughout the attack. When police found him, he had a swastika crudely carved into his forehead. A week later my son-in-law, one James Jennings, was arrested for the senseless attack. He had been bragging about it to a number of people, and following his capture, went on to tell the police he was proud of what he had done. His only regret was that he hadn't finished the job.

I finally got my laughter under control. "You know, I never noticed the color of your eyes. They are sort of green, aren't they?" I answered my own question. "Yes, green, like the grass. Do you like looking at grass, Jennings?" A glimmer of understanding ran through his face. In that split second, he spit; a ball of his reeking mucus-infused saliva came toward me in slow motion. I didn't bother ducking or trying to evade it. The filthy wetness splattered under my nose and across my mouth, dribbling down to my chin. His faint smile disappeared in a hurry when I spit back, returning the infectious saliva to its original source. I shook his hand. "That, Jennings, is to thank you for your donation. You are misunderstood. You felt guilty about that poor victim who was attacked and how that unfortunate boy didn't deserve the treatment to which you had subjected him. And here you are volunteering your eyes, your very own green eyes, so another, less fortunate sole than yourself, will be given the precious gift of sight. You simply want this little wrong to be righted." Sweat beads poured down Jennings' hairless head, landing rapidly, haphazardly, one on top of the other into the hastily carved openings in the bedroom floor, collateral damage caused by the tank. "Can you believe this is your lucky day? You look skeptical, asshole, but fear not, I'm going to explain everything. Listen carefully with your newly cleaned out ear passages. Because now, when I remove your eyes, I'm going to be very careful about it. You are going to be an eye donor, Jennings. Isn't that great? Most eye donors wait until they are dead, but not you, you are different. Originally, I had planned to simply rip your eyes from their sockets and stuff them down your throat. I mean, after all, do you really need your eyes? Are you even using them? I know you sat through the Holocaust class and watched all of the films, but did you really see anything? My guess is, no. But the beautiful green of your eyes and the thought that you've volunteered to donate them changes everything. Fortunately for you, I have a little surgical training, albeit with animals, but as you are sort of a rabid animal yourself, things are really falling into, or should I say, out of place? I told you this was your lucky day!" The stupid fuck had the dumbest look I had ever seen.

There he was, in the news again. He said he had no regrets for brutally assaulting an innocent bystander. I watched the news with disgust. The article made reference to the initial acts of vandalism at the cemetery. It described how three of the original four arrested had turned their lives around. One had become a policeman. Talk about a turn of fortune! Not our Mr. Jennings, however. Apparently, he had not learned anything from his mandatory community service and history lesson. He was back at it. Some people are just plain no good, like the legal system. The louse met bail and was out on the streets yet again. Did Rachel have anything to do with posting bail?

"Let me tell you my original plan, the one I had for your eyes before discovering someone else has a use for them. I love shish kabob. How about you? Oh, never mind. I have these two skewers. I was going to plunge them, one at a time, directly into your eyes. Sort of like spearing a fish or an olive from a martini glass, and I had planned to maneuver your eyes onto the middle of the skewer. You like meat, right? I figured we could find some mouse or rat meat from this slime of a rat-hole you call home, and spear them as well. Just for kicks, I was going to add green olives to the skewer. My little joke because they remind me so much of eyeballs. Green eyes. Then, since you wouldn't be able to see too well, I was going to help feed you by shoving the entire feast, skewer and all down your worthless throat. But, plans change. You'd know all about that." The poor bastard, I thought to myself for the briefest of seconds. *Instead, I carefully removed the cork from the scalpel's tip, and with a surgeon's precision, sliced skin, tissue and muscle, finally severing the optic nerves before removing Jennings' eyes. Smiling, I looked at his face. His mouth was "O" shaped. It matched the two gaping black holes where his eyes were once housed. I found a flashlight, shined it back and forth between the two empty eye sockets, hoping this might permit some light to penetrate the dark recesses of his brain. "Snakes' eyes are like glass eyes. They never close," I told him. "Now, your eyes will never close." I placed the eyes on ice, protected by a snap-topped plastic container. "That is a tremendous donation you just made, sir, if I may say so myself," I hissed. "Some lucky recipient will have an entire new world open up to them, thanks to your generosity. What have you to say to that, kind*

sir?" The bastard spit at me again, and that's when the idea hit me. No sense putting the unused skewers to waste. I began talking to Jennings about birth control. Despite his condition, I could see he was still obstinate. "The last thing we want is one of your filthy offspring running around wild. The Nazis believed in sterilization. So do I." I pointed the tip of the skewer in front of his sightless face and then slowly lowered it downward. I grabbed a sledgehammer, the same ones used by the Nazis November 9, 1938. He sensed what I was doing, which thrilled me. Like a trapped animal, his entire body went rigid. I wasted no time striking the sledgehammer down hard on the skewer's end and deep into the bulls-eye hole in Jennings' manhood! He collapsed. The cherry was on the sundae.

The birth of my granddaughter was one of the most difficult days on earth. I had hoped against hope Rachel would see Jennings for the rat shit human waste he was and leave him forever. Hell, not all my prayers are answered. She was committed to him, and now, after having given birth, planned a long life together.

My wife was perched in front of the tube, totally engrossed in some vacuous reality show. Television isn't my thing. I sat with an old Mickey Spillane paperback that read just as well now as fifty years prior when freshly displayed on drugstore racks. I needed something to keep my mind occupied, distracted from thoughts of making my daughter a widow. Rachel and what's his name were out to dinner and a movie. I acquiesced for a Saturday night, one-half of a baby-sitting team. I should be a saint. Upstairs, I heard our granddaughter cry out. I hated to put the book down. Mike Hammer was kicking ass. I looked at my wife, but she was oblivious to everything but that insipid show. "Do you want me to go up and see what's wrong?" I asked her.

"What? What's wrong?"

I shook my head. "Forget it. I'm going upstairs. I heard Eva cry. Probably dropped the pacifier or something." It's a good thing I didn't wait for her response, for none was forthcoming.

The nightlight was on, but I flicked on the table lamp as well. "Here now, what's the matter? Let grandpa take a look." Then Rachel's words stormed back to me. It was the first time I had met my grandchild. "She's adorable. She looks just like her father. She has her father's eyes!" It was there, in her eyes, inbred hatred passed down from her old man. The Star of David dangled from my neck, touched her chin. She grabbed at the Shield and yanked it off its chain. Then, a toothless grin and a wink, it was something that had to be excised. I removed the pen from my shirt pocket and jabbed twice. Hard. There were dark, bloody holes where her eyes had been. She shrieked. I heard my wife race up the stairs.

From the doorway, she took one look, paled. "What the hell have you done? How could you?"

"It was easy," I said.

Bruce Harris is the author of *Sherlock Holmes and Doctor Watson: ABout Type,* published by The Battered Silicon Dispatch Box.
His short stories have been published in numerous online journals and print anthologies. "Swing Me," which appears in the 2010 anthology *Bloody Carnival,* was nominated for a Pushcart Prize.

DARK MATTER

B.D. Prince

Paulie Shoemaker sensed there was something wrong with the new house the moment he entered. That skin-crawly feeling you're being watched. He wasn't sure if his parents sensed it, but he suspected the realtor had; the way she kept glancing over her shoulder while giving the tour. Paulie felt it again carrying the last box upstairs, wishing his brother Max had waited for him. He resisted peeking over his shoulder until the second floor landing.

The stairs were empty.

Paulie looked forward to sharing a room with his big brother, despite the new house's extra bedroom. That would be the baby's when she came. At least Mom thought it would be a she. He hoped for a little brother to play with when Max abandoned him to play with his friends.

The hot, stagnant air struck him as he entered his room, early afternoon sun glaring through the undraped windows. He opened the box and discovered his baseball glove. "Hey Max, wanna play catch?"

"You'll have to find my glove first."

Paulie read Max's lips. He'd developed the habit after losing most his hearing at age four from a double ear infection. Fortunately, hearing aids made lip-reading unnecessary. Like now – he could hear someone walking above them.

Max stood on his tiptoes stacking board games onto the closet's top shelf. A loud THUMP above them startled Max, landing him on his rear, game pieces scattering across the floor.

Paulie jumped. "You okay?"

"Yeah," grumbled Max.

"What is Dad doing on the roof?"

Max shrugged, dusted himself off, and tried opening the window. Years of paint layers made the sash nearly impossible to budge. Paulie hurried to help, struggling with the other side until the window finally gave way with a creak.

Max leaned out the window, peering at the roof. "Dad, what are you doing up there?"

"Up where?" Dad called back, carrying a box in front of the house. Startled, Max gawked at his father below.

"Never mind," Paulie shouted.

Retreating inside, Max stared at the ceiling.

"What?" Paulie asked.

"Nothing. Just help me pick these up."

Paulie considered asking Max about the noise they heard above them, but decided he didn't want to know.

Paulie awoke with a start, sitting bolt upright, wide-eyed, listening. Shuffling sounds.

He pulled the covers up to his chin.

"Max," he whispered. No response.

"Max!" he repeated louder. Still nothing.

A swath of moonlight shone across Max's turned-down covers. He was gone. But Paulie wasn't alone.

Something struck the wall. "MAX," Paulie cried, his voice rising in pitch. He felt frantically around the nightstand, unable to find his hearing aids. Checking his ears he realized he hadn't taken them out. THUMP. Was something trying to get in?

There – a shadow crept along the wall. A prowler? The Boogeyman? Was Max already captured? Or eaten? He started to cry.

The dark mass rustled in the corner. Paulie held his breath.

Brief silence. Then the sound of running water. Was it raining? No, the sound came from inside the room. His mind raced, envisioning the walls bleeding like in that late-night Creature Feature he and Max watched.

"Max! MAX!"

The shadowy figure turned. The wet sound dribbled to a stop.

"Max?"

Paulie's brother was sleepwalking again. Sleep-peeing, actually. With the anxiety of moving and leaving his friends, Paulie could understand why Max's midnight wandering might return.

When he snapped out of it, Max made Paulie swear he wouldn't tell. After changing into a pair of sweat pants, Max used his pajama bottoms to mop up the urine then climbed back into bed. The room fell silent.

Max snickered.

"What's so funny?"

"I dreamt we were at our old house and I couldn't find the bathroom."

"Looks like you found it to me," Paulie laughed. Then they both giggled themselves to sleep.

The baseball hit Paulie's glove with a loud smack. "Ow, not so hard."

Despite his stinging palm, he was happy to be outside in the fresh air instead of the stuffy bedroom unpacking. Mostly he liked having his big brother all to himself.

Max resented moving, leaving his friends behind. Paulie didn't mind. He didn't have any real friends back there anyway. Plus now, Max played with him again. Their four year difference hadn't mattered when they were younger; they played together all the time. But Max somehow got older, only wanted to play with friends his age. Or maybe just got tired of explaining why his little brother talked funny.

Paulie lobbed the ball back and smiled. Today he didn't worry about being picked last, or not at all.

The baseball whizzed past Paulie's ear, knocking his hearing aid to the ground. Dropping his glove, he cupped his ear.

"Ma-ax!"

"It's not my fault you can't catch."

Paulie searched until he found his hearing aid a few feet behind him. While inserting the device, he glimpsed a shadow moving in the attic window. When he pointed it out to Max, the shadow was gone.

"Don't be so paranoid," Max said, "It's probably just Dad."

"That's what you said yesterday."

Paulie tried to keep his eye on the ball but couldn't shake that skin-crawly feeling of being watched.

After dinner the boys sat on their bedroom floor playing checkers. Paulie jumped two of Max's men, landing on the last row.

"King me."

"I'll crown you, all right," Max mumbled.

"I can read your lips, you know."

Max extended his middle finger. "How are you at sign language?"

After a moment, they burst out laughing.

Their laughter faded hearing work boots clomping down the hall, stopping outside their room. They waited for Dad to open the door. He didn't.

Paulie whispered to Max, "What's he doing out there?"

Max shrugged, crept to the half-open doorway, and listened. He mouthed he heard someone breathing then motioned for Paulie to stay put. Slowly grasping the door handle he swung it open and jumped into the hallway.

Paulie quickly joined him. It felt like entering a walk-in freezer. He rubbed his arms, ironing out the gooseflesh. They could see their breath but no one else. Puzzled, the boys searched the entire upstairs but failed to find another living soul.

After breakfast Paulie searched for Max, but he wasn't in the house or backyard. Opening the front door he spied Max wheeling his red mountain bike from the garage.

"Wait, Max, I'll come with you."

Max hesitated. "All right. But hurry up."

Paulie ran into the garage while Max circled impatiently, As Paulie coasted up on his Schwinn, Max pedaled off, his shoulder-length hair fluttering like a tattered flag. Paulie struggled to keep up. Rounding the block, they surveyed the neighborhood, spotting two boys ambling along the sidewalk, talking.

Max jammed on his brake, laying a long patch of rubber, skidding to a stop beside them. Paulie braked, swerving to avoid Max, nearly falling.

Max broke the ice. "What's up?"

The tall, lanky kid with spiked blond hair and a large hooked nose answered, "You new around here?"

"Just moved in a couple days ago. I'm Max."

"Garrett." He gestured toward his square-jawed friend with the unruly mop of brown hair. "This is Scott."

Garrett asked, "Who's the runt?"

"That's just my little brother."

Paulie gave a small wave.

After an awkward pause Max said, "Guess we'll see you around."

Garrett smirked. "Unless we see you first."

Max sped off leaving Paulie to catch up.

Amanda Shoemaker carefully climbed the stairs to put her sons to bed. She wouldn't make this climb much longer the way her ankles were swelling, the baby nearly full term. But she determined to tuck them in and kiss them goodnight as long as possible.

"Time for bed," she said, entering the boys' room.

Tired from riding bikes all day, they were already in bed. She kissed Max's forehead then leaned over Paulie, checking his ears.

"You forgot to take your hearing aids out."

Paulie yawned, handing them to his mom to place on the nightstand. Tucking the covers under his chin, she kissed his forehead and smiled. "Sweet dreams. Don't forget to say your prayers."

Mrs. Shoemaker left the door ajar, afraid she wouldn't hear them call during the night.

In the hallway a shiver grabbed her. She poked her head back in the boy's room. "It's awful drafty up here; sure you wouldn't like an extra blanket?"

"We're fine Mom," Max said, yawning.

"Okay, sleep tight."

Rubbing her arms, she headed down the hall. A floorboard creaked behind her.

"Change your mind about that blanket?" She turned, but the hallway was empty. Shrugging, she continued toward the stairs. A heavier set of footfalls echoed hers. Fear gripped her stomach. She convinced herself that the sound was just an echo from the hardwood floor. She paused atop the staircase. The heavy footfalls continued. Once. Twice. The hairs on the back of her neck bristled. If she turned, she'd be indulging her irrational fears. Or worse, confirming them.

Someone exhaled behind her. An arctic blast gripped her neck in its

144

icy clutch.

She spun to confront her pursuer, heels teetering on the edge of the top step. She wind-milled her arms desperately to maintain balance; then pitched backward.

Airborne seemingly for an eternity, Amanda grasped at the air before slamming head first into the stairs. Her body jackknifed, flipping facedown. Her chin caught step after step, teeth slamming together; lightning bolts flashing inside her head with each hammer-strike of her jaw. As gravity dragged her down, steps raked at her abdomen as if trying to dig out her unborn child. Darkness enveloped her.

Startled by the commotion, the boys bolted into the hall. Skidding to a stop at the landing, they stared aghast at their mother's motionless body at the bottom of the stairs.

"Mommy!" Paulie cried.

Dad bounded into view downstairs. He scowled at the boys, accusingly. Kneeling, he gently rolled his wife onto her back.

Seeing her bloody grimace sucked the air out of Paulie. He descended a step.

"Stay there!" Dad yelled.

Max jerked him back.

Dad tentatively checked her neck for a pulse.

Paulie prayed, "Please don't be dead, please."

Dad retrieved a cell phone from his pocket and dialed. A faint woman's voice answered, "9-1-1, what's your emergency?"

Paulie brushed his teeth in the upstairs bathroom, grateful his mother was home from the hospital, but still worried. He couldn't believe she lost the baby. Dad insisted they not mention it around her. Since coming home, all she did was sleep. Although his father never said it, Paulie felt like he blamed him and Max for the accident.

A hollow thud echoed above him. He stopped, listening.

"You boys keep it down up there," Dad shouted from downstairs over the distant din of the television.

Paulie rinsed and spat. Reaching for the doorknob, a louder thump rattled the medicine cabinet.

"I SAID, KEEP IT DOWN. YOUR MOTHER'S TRYING TO REST."

Easing the door open, Paulie peeked down the hall. Empty. He tiptoed into the hallway. Halfway down the corridor a trapdoor in the ceiling hung open like the jaw of some giant beast, waiting to devour him.

Why hadn't he noticed it earlier? Perhaps it wasn't open before. Then why is it open now? A voice inside him answered, BECAUSE IT'S HUNGRY.

He wished Max were here.

Paulie decided to sneak up to the trapdoor then dart underneath, not stopping until safely in his room. Cautiously approaching, the hallway seemed to lengthen. Reaching the gaping trapdoor, it suddenly slammed shut, startling Paulie onto his rear.

"THAT'S IT!" Paulie's dad stomped up the stairs.

Panicked, Paulie bolted for his bedroom, praying he'd arrive first. He ducked into his room just as Dad's head appeared.

He shoved the door open. "WHAT'S GOING ON UP HERE?"

The boys exchanged glances and shrugs.

"I told you boys to keep it down."

"It wasn't us. There's something in the attic," Paulie said.

"You're saying mice made that racket?"

Max said, "Or a big-ass raccoon."

"Or a smart-ass kid," Dad said, staring them down. "If I have to come up here again I'm getting the paddle."

As Dad turned to leave, the trapdoor clattered down the hall. He glanced at the boys then left to investigate.

The boys quickly followed. Silence. About to give up, they heard the trapdoor rattle directly above them. Startled, they looked up. A rope with a ball knotted at the end swung from the trapdoor like a hangman's noose.

Dad grasped the rope. "You'd better stand back."

The boys retreated. With a loud rush the retractable ladder plummeted from the ceiling, slamming against the floor.

Paulie jumped. Staring at the black maw in the ceiling, something in the attic creaked. Cold air descended, carrying a flurry of dust. Dad cautiously mounted the ladder until the attic swallowed him up.

After an eternity in the belly of the attic, the silence broke with a click. Blackness evaporated into the sallow glow of a bare light bulb swinging from the rafters. Their father loomed over the opening, his shadow pendulating across the floor. Then he disappeared.

Max climbed high enough to poke his head inside the attic. "Whoa..."

"What is it?" Paulie asked.

"You gotta see this."

Thick dust carpeted the attic floor. Dad and Max left a trail like footprints in fresh snow. The naked bulb painted twisted shadows across the bare walls. The previous owner left behind a steamer trunk and stacks of boxes. Nobody had been up here for ages.

Before they could explore for hidden treasures, a faint voice interrupted.

"Honey?" Mom called. "Where is everyone?"

Concern clouded Dad's expression. "C'mon boys, let's explore the attic another time."

"Yeah," Paulie said, "daytime."

Paulie forgot how much he enjoyed rainy days—the paradiddle rhythm on the roof; booming, resonating thunder you could feel; days spent indoors with family. Since Max discovered new friends his age, he was hardly home anymore. Except today. If the rain continued they could play checkers or backgammon or crazy-eights all day. Maybe even Monopoly.

He hoped it never stopped raining.

Max tired of their third game of backgammon after Paulie rolled his fourth pair of double-sixes. He was outrunning Max, all his men safely inside his home board.

A clatter reverberated down the hallway.

Since visiting the attic, the unexplained noises increased; or Paulie just became more aware of them. Dad said you had to expect creaks and groans from old, drafty houses built in the 1930s.

"Hey," Max exclaimed, "let's check out the attic!"

Paulie's eyes widened. They'd talked about exploring it before but Max hadn't brought it up lately and Paulie sure wasn't going to.

"W-we haven't finished our game."

"You win." Max hurried into the hall. "C'mon."

Thunder rumbled overhead, rattling the attic trapdoor. Max stretched, grasped the dangling rope, and yanked. Paulie leapt back as the ladder slammed to the floor.

They listened. No reaction from Mom. Dad was at work. The only sounds were the howling wind and driving rain.

Paulie waited while Max searched for the light switch pull-string. Suddenly, the bare 60-watt bulb blinked to life like a single jaundiced eye. The bulb, dangling from heavy gauge wire, cast swaying shadows around the attic as Paulie peeked in. Dust motes drifted through the air like snowflakes.

Paulie started for the steamer trunk but Max got there first. Before opening, Max grinned darkly. "What if there's a body in there?"

He let Max open it.

Inside they discovered coats, handbags, scarves, but no body. Exploring the attic further, they discovered boxes of jackets, hats, purses, plus a dozen umbrellas leaning against a wall next to a row of briefcases.

Unable to find any magic lamps or vintage baseball cards in the boxes, Paulie surveyed the attic for other items of interest. As he neared the wall his shadow became darker, more distinct. For fun, Paulie made a shadow-bunny hop across the wall until it ran into another shadow, a shadow sporting an old cabbie hat like James Cagney wore in those black and white movies Dad always watched.

He turned, expecting to see Max donning a hat from the trunk. He wasn't. Paulie examined the shadow. It still appeared to be wearing a hat.

He glanced at Max. Long hair but no hat.

"What're you looking at?" Max asked. Approaching the wall his shadow solidified next to Paulie's.

Now there were three.

Max recoiled, glancing over both shoulders, but nobody was there. The brothers gawked at the man-sized shadow anomaly, confused, curious, unsettled.

Then it moved.

Both boys whirled and bolted, nearly bypassing the ladder, neither stopping until they were safely behind their locked bedroom door.

"What the hell was that?" Max said.

His heart pounding, Paulie could only shake his head.

They debated what could've caused the third shadow, eventually convincing themselves it wasn't anything uncanny, just a shadowy illusion.

"The light!" Paulie exclaimed. They'd both been too busy running for their lives to turn it off. But if they left it on, Dad would know they'd been up there.

Paulie shadowed Max as they crept up the ladder. Oddly, instead of pulling the string and running away, Max seemed drawn to the spot where they'd seen the strange, silhouette.

The shadow was still there.

The boys cautiously flanked it, waiting for it to move.

They weren't disappointed.

The shadow turned toward Max and then Paulie, as if sizing them up. Paulie couldn't believe his eyes. Max leaned in.

"He's saying something," Max said, studying the oily-black figure. "Watch, when he turns his head... right there!

Paulie stared, moving his lips in silent conversation.

The shadow gestured with its hand.

"Can you tell what it's saying?" Max asked.

Eyes wet with fear, Paulie whispered, "It's saying, 'Come closer.'"

The next day the rain subsided. Max couldn't wait to play show-and-tell. His friends all reacted the same way – they ran, screaming like little girls. Eventually, curiosity brought everyone back. Once initiated, his friends brought others to scare, acting all brave, yet never getting too close. It became a rite of passage, an initiation into an elite club – *the shadow-man scared the crap outta me* club.

As summer progressed, the novelty wore off. One afternoon, despite stifling heat, Max and friends sat around the attic wearing hats scavenged from the dusty trunk. Larry used a lady's scarf to dab sweat from his eyes and pudgy, pink cheeks.

Slim-Jim reclined against some boxes, slack-jawed. Scott's head bobbed. Paulie doodled a smiley face on the dusty floor.

"Let's get outta here," Garrett said, "this is boring."

Max reacted as if he'd been slapped. Before Garrett took two steps

Max blurted, "Sure you're not just scared?"

Garrett spun around. "Listen Maxine, I ain't scared of nothing."

"Then why're you running away?"

"Bet I can get closer to it than you, wuss!"

"Wanna bet?"

Scott jumped in, "I'd beat you both by a mile."

The challenge was on.

They drew names from a hat to see who could get closest to touching the shadow-man. Paulie volunteered to manage the hat.

Nobody was bored now.

Paulie selected the first name. Scott took several deep breaths, gathering up his courage. The others goaded him, clucking like chickens. Finally, Scott sprinted toward the shadow, tagged the wall, missing by three feet, then bolted back.

Larry charged like an elephant, yelling the entire way, missing the wall by a country mile. Slim-Jim tip-toed to the shadow, closed his eyes, touched nothing but air, then pirouetted, leaping away like a gangly ballet dancer. Garrett came closest, holding the record until Max's turn.

Max inched toward the wall as the others taunted. A board creaked underfoot. He glanced back at Paulie.

Paulie mouthed, "NO!"

He advanced within arm's reach. Their shadows touched. The jeering stopped. The attic became eerily silent, like the earth suddenly stopped turning.

The shadow-man's lips moved again. Paulie shouted, "Don't do it, Max!"

Max sucked in a slow, nervous breath; then like a fencer thrusting his foil, he lunged, poking the shadow-man in the chest. Turning, he examined his fingers in disbelief.

Paulie gasped as incorporeal hands reached out of the wall, clutching at his brother's back. Max strutted forward, narrowly eluding the shadow-man's grasp.

Larry and Slim-Jim rushed to high-five Max.

Paulie finally exhaled. "Congratulations, Max."

Garrett interrupted, "Challenge ain't over yet."

"What're you talking about," Max said. "I won fair and square."

Larry said, "Yeah, Garrett. Max touched him; I saw it."

Paulie felt Garrett walk up behind him and say, "It ain't over until *everybody* goes."

"Everybody went already," Max said.

Garrett bumped Paulie from behind. "Not everybody."

The oxygen left the room. Paulie turned, facing Garrett. "I-I-I'm not playing."

Garrett stepped forward. "What's the matter? Scaredy cat?"

Paulie backed toward the wall. "I-I'm not scared."

Garrett advanced. "Don't you wanna be in the club?"

Could Garrett really mean it, about joining their club? And if so, could he muster the courage to confront the shadow-man?

Paulie and Garrett continued their tango, Garrett grinning, glancing over Paulie's shoulder. Goosebumps erupted as he realized what Garrett was doing.

Max shouted, "Look out, Paulie!"

Paulie spun and found himself staring into a man-shaped abyss. The tenebrous shadow drew him in as if he teetered on the edge of a black hole. Helplessly transfixed, Paulie watched the inky-black specter reach for him.

His lips silently pleaded with the shadow-man not to hurt him. Its sudden icy-hot touch awakened him from his trance. Paulie gaped as his body absorbed the shadow-man's hand. Gradually, the shadowy appendage solidified into ashen flesh. The energy drained from Paulie's legs as blackness enveloped him, a scream frozen in his throat.

Gradually rising from the depths of a bottomless black lake, Paulie heard distant voices beyond the water's horizon. Nearing the surface, the world became brighter, sounds more distinct.

Paulie awoke to laughter.

"Oh, man. That was priceless!" Scott laughed, wiping his eyes. Max and Larry helped Paulie up. Dazed, Paulie smiled and asked, "Did I make it? Am I in the club?"

Garrett said, "Sorry, kid. No bedwetters allowed."

Paulie's heart sank discovering the dark stain in his trousers.

Lying awake, Paulie stared at the ceiling, the bedroom stained with bleak, moonlit shadows. Max tossed restlessly in the bed beside him. The attic commotion was unusually animated; floorboards creaking, frenetic pounding; as if the shadow-man was trying to break free. Had he tasted something, or someone, that whetted his appetite and now craved more?

Paulie examined his abdomen, the red handprint still tender to the touch. The image of the tar-like hand reaching out of the wall flashed in his mind. The attic trapdoor rattled as if the shadow-man read his thoughts. Paulie pulled the covers up to his eyeballs.

Try as he might to keep vigil, sleep eventually overtook him, filling Paulie's head with visions of the cold, dark stranger.

Paulie startled awake, heart racing, glancing from shadow to shadow, expecting each to be Him.

The room was still.

Suddenly, a noise. Footsteps? Or just his adrenaline-stoked heartbeat?

153

Paulie desperately felt around the nightstand for his hearing aids, knocking one to the floor. Locating the other he frantically shoved it in.

And listened.

Footsteps outside the bedroom door.

Paulie turned but Max's bed was empty. Could he be sleepwalking again? He inspected every shadow. No sign of Max. Paulie cranked his hearing aid up, listening carefully. Footfalls echoed down the hall.

A surge of panic struck him, remembering his mother's near fatal plunge. He bolted out the door and scrambled down the hall, catching Max by the shoulder right before he stepped over the edge.

Paulie tried to shake him from his sleep-like trance. "Max, wake up!" But the harder Paulie fought to corral him, the harder he resisted. What was wrong with him? It was like he was trying to escape.

Finally he spun free, sticking his crooked nose right in Paulie's face. Paulie gasped seeing the James Cagney scowl, his skin gray in the midnight gloom. It wasn't Max. It was the shadow-man. Only, he wasn't a shadow. He was flesh and bone.

Paulie gaped, petrified by the malevolent glare. In that moment they exchanged a tacit agreement. Paulie let go.

The glowering man tugged the brim of his cabbie hat firmly over his furrowed brow, turned, then bounded off into the night.

Paulie lingered atop the stairs, a dull pounding in his ears growing louder, like frantic fists hammering on his skull. Then it ceased. Paulie emerged from his stupor and wandered back to his bedroom. Max's empty bed haunted him like a recurring nightmare.

The muffled pounding returned, only, not just in his head. But if the shadow-man just materialized and escaped, then where's the ruckus coming from? It must be a nightmare. If he just climbed back into bed, it would all cease.

Shuffling to his bed, he smacked his shin on the bedpost. He grabbed his leg, cursing under his breath. Then it struck him, like someone pinching themselves to determine if they were dreaming. The pain... he must be awake!

154

More pounding. Could it be coming from the attic, he wondered?

Paulie limped into the hall. The attic steps were down. The light was out.

"Max?"

No response.

Paulie hobbled back to his room, retrieving a flashlight. No matter how many times he'd set foot in the attic, it always sent a stab of fear though his chest. And those times he hadn't gone alone. Or at night.

He called again, louder. A series of pounds seemed to answer. He climbed the steps, legs trembling.

The pitch-black attic swallowed him whole. The flashlight beam wavered. He swung his free hand hoping to find the light switch string. It brushed his hand. Grasping it, he pulled.

The bare bulb flared to life, temporarily blinding him. The pounding intensified. Paulie wondered if Max sleepwalked his way up here, stumbled into the trunk, and the lid slammed shut, trapping him inside.

The ghost flare gradually faded from his vision, revealing the trunk, lid open. No Max. Maybe he sleepwalked into a corner again. Probing the murky corners with the pale flashlight beam, something caught Paulie's eye.

A shadow danced on the wall, jumping and waving its arms. He'd never seen the shadow-man this animated before.

As he approached the shadow, its flailing subsided. But something was different. Its shape was shorter, thinner, the familiar cabbie hat replaced by shoulder length hair. Could there be another?

Edging closer, Paulie sensed the shadow trying to communicate. It gestured as if trying to describe something.

"I don't understand."

The shadow repeated the pantomime.

Paulie shook his head.

The shadow's shoulders slumped. Then, in apparent frustration, the shadow thrust out its middle finger.

"Max!" Paulie shouted in disbelief. "But, how?"

Max's shadow gestured again.

"Slow down," Paulie said, "I can't understand you."

Max's shadow motioned him closer.

Closer...

Suddenly shadow-hands seized Paulie by the shoulders. The icy-hot pain was incredible, like the time he nearly got frostbite and his hands were freezing yet felt like they were on fire.

Paulie struggled to escape his brother's icy clench, the pain spreading down his arms. He stared in horror as Max's shadow-hands solidified, black shadow becoming gray flesh.

"Max, no!"

In a rush of adrenaline-fueled panic, Paulie wrenched himself from shadow-Max's clutches, tumbling to the floor.

Paulie sat and rocked, rubbing his shoulders.

Max's shadow pleaded with him.

"No, Max, I can't," he cried. "I just can't."

Shadow-Max dropped to his knees, begging.

Paulie covered his face, sobbing. "I'm sorry, Max. I'm so sorry."

It was a long, restless night. Shadows tormented Paulie's dreams. Each time he awoke he found Max's bed empty, the nightmare still alive.

Sitting down to breakfast, Paulie supported his head with one hand, drowsily spooning cereal into his mouth with the other.

His mother wiped a dishrag across the table. "You boys stay up late last night?"

Paulie perked up. "W-why do you think that?"

"I heard you wrestling up there. Plus, you can barely hold your head up," she said.

"We were just... talking."

"Oh? What were you two chatting about so late?"

Paulie studied his cereal. "I-I don't know, just stuff."

"Is your brother up yet?"

Paulie dropped his spoon.

"I, uh…" <u>Think, Paulie, Think!</u> He quickly shoveled three spoonfuls of cereal into his mouth and mumbled, "I'll go check."

Rushing from the kitchen, Paulie wondered how he'd explain Max's disappearance. He could say Max ran away. No, then she'd want to look for him. What if he told her Max snuck out early to play with friends? Paulie smiled. But what happens when Max doesn't come home for dinner? His smile faded.

As he reached the stairs someone knocked on the front door. He froze. What if it's one of Max's friends?

"Paulie, can you get the door?" Mom called from the kitchen.

"Sure, Mom." He prayed it wasn't for Max.

They knocked again.

Paulie opened the door. It was Garrett.

"Is Max home?"

Paulie just gawked.

"I SAID," Garrett shouted, over-enunciating each syllable, "IS YOUR BRO-THER HOME?" Then under his breath, "You know, the normal one."

Paulie narrowed his gaze, nodded.

"Well?"

He stepped aside, letting Garrett in, then led him upstairs. Reaching Paulie's room, Garrett looked inside. "Where's Max?"

Paulie continued down the hall to the retractable attic stairs and pointed. Garrett brushed by and climbed into the attic, calling for Max. Scanning the attic, Garrett asked, "Where's your stupid brother?"

Paulie headed deeper into the attic.

"I asked you a question, retard."

Paulie proceeded to the shadow wall.

"What are you, deaf *and* dumb?" Garrett poked him in the chest. "Do

157

you know where your stupid brother is or not?"

Paulie pointed at the shadow.

"So? I've seen it before, you know," Garrett said. "Besides, it's getting boring."

He pointed again, raising his eyebrows for emphasis.

"What?" Garrett examined the shadow. Then his head cocked.

Paulie stepped back.

"Wait..." Garrett said, "He looks... different." He turned but Paulie wasn't there. He was behind Garrett now. Garrett spun. Paulie shoved him as hard as he could.

Garrett flew backward into Max's awaiting grasp. Instead of bouncing off the wall, Garrett sank into it, like someone plunging into a murky lake, instantly enveloped by black tentacles. Max grappled with Garrett, pulling him into the wall. Garrett's upper torso faded to black; Max's arms became flesh. Max's head materialized from the wall as he sucked in a rasping breath then was jerked back into the shadows.

The two writhed together, their bodies alternating between flesh and shadow, screams fading in and out.

Paulie waited helplessly.

Finally, one of them emerged.

It was Garrett.

Garrett crawled toward him, grasping for Paulie's ankle, only to fall short, yanked back to the wall, his fingernails clawing bloody grooves across the dusty floorboards. Garrett scrabbled forward, Max struggling to pull him back in, but Garrett was too strong. He reached out to Paulie for help.

Paulie kicked him in the face.

Garrett's eyes rolled back in his head before his face kissed the floor. Max's shadow pulled Garrett's boneless body back into the wall. As the last of Garrett dissolved into shadow, the color drained from his face.

Suddenly Max tumbled to the floor, gasping for air.

"Max!" Paulie cried, wrapping his arms around him.

Max trembled in his arms as they rocked and wept, Max repeating,

"I'm so cold, so cold."

Paulie hardly slept the next few nights, between his guilty conscience and the restless attic dweller. Max made him swear never to enter the attic again or tell another soul what they'd done.

He kept his promise, even when the police came around asking questions. Even when they were recruited for the search party scouring nearby woods, ditches, and culverts.

By fall the fliers, once posted on nearly every telephone pole, had disappeared. "Missing" posters taped in store windows faded like most people's memories of the lost teen. Even the noises in the attic subsided.

The quietude lasted until early December. Sprawled on the living room floor, the boys' Saturday morning cartoons were interrupted by loud thumps, then scuffling sounds upstairs. Paulie glanced nervously at Max.

Mom entered from the kitchen wiping her hands with a dishtowel. "Boys, can you go upstairs and give your father a hand? Sounds like he could use your help with the Christmas decorations."

The boys shared an anxious look.

Another loud thud sounded like Dad jumped down from the attic, followed by scurrying footsteps. The boys chuckled, imagining their father's reaction to seeing the shadow-man come to life.

Paulie hurried to the stairs to witness his dad's expression as he bounded down the steps. Suddenly he was bowled over, the breath knocked out of him. He struggled to his feet just as Garrett scrambled for the exit, skin gray, looking like he'd just stepped out of a black and white movie.

As Garrett fumbled the doorknob he yelled, "Y-you two are dead meat! Y-you hear me? Dead!"

Then he was gone, the front door hanging open. An icy gust blew in a handful of dead leaves.

"What was all that racket?" their mother asked. "I thought I asked you to go help your father."

Paulie looked at Max, pondering how they might do that.

B.D. Prince was born in Michigan - a dark fiction and comedy writer who credits these proclivities to the fact that as a child he could see a cemetery from his bedroom window and that he was born with a freakishly long funny bone. He moved to California in 1990 to pursue screenwriting and get a tan. Bryan has written everything from screenplays to greeting cards to one-liners for Joan Rivers. He is currently pursuing his passion for writing short fiction and completing his first novel.

You can find Bryan on Facebook at www.facebook.com/bryan.prince.52

BONUS STORY

The Eye Is the Mirror

Allan Rozinski

The boy appeared normal – unremarkable, actually – in every respect save one. And if one were to remark about what made him so remarkably unremarkable, one might say no feature drew or held one's attention – except one, that is.

His hair was dark and straight; skin, largely unblemished and almost pale; and his frame tended toward spare, but not excessively so. He was the kind of boy who, if no special talents should become evident – nothing in a facility for using language or numbers in innovative ways, or in the development of an exceptional athletic skill or musical talent – would simply fade into oblivion, into a sea of undistinguished faces attached to invisible lives amidst the stark gray background of human life as it was.

Yes, he was unremarkable in every way, really – except for that eye.

Lest this account give you cause to believe I am going to insult your intelligence by implying the boy possessed that superstitious cliché known as *ocularus sinister* – the "evil eye" – let me assure you I place no significance whatsoever on the fact the … aberration … involved his left eye rather than the right. But what needs to be determined is both the cause as well as the ultimate effect of that eye, given its wholly alien quality in the context of human experience. However, instead I fear more drastic measures are required to protect humanity.

Radha Mali walked up to me in my classroom during open house – an event scheduled about two months into each new school year to which parents were invited to meet with teachers after school to discuss their children's academic status. She wore jeans, a loose-fitting blouse, and flat, black shoes. A dark wool coat was cradled in her arm. He walked in behind her and wandered over to the windows.

"Mr. Jameson?" she said.

"Call me Bill," I said, offering a hand. She shook it listlessly.

"I am Radha Mali. My son Shivin is in your class. How is he doing?"

"He's doing fine," I said. The truth was I had some concerns about Shivin. I didn't know how to tactfully broach those issues with her, nor if it was appropriate for me to bring them up yet, since Shivin had only been in my classroom for a week.

However, the sight of her rumpled, wrinkled clothes; tousled, unkempt hair; and blotchy, sallow skin gave me further cause to worry about Shivin's welfare. Her sunken eyes and cheeks and haggard appearance led me to suspect she was either a drug abuser or afflicted by a serious medical condition. Yet the most disturbing trait was an affliction characterized by small, intermittent facial tics and occasional twitches of her body.

I remembered scanning the historical information in Shivin's file when he arrived in my class. The contents of his file indicated he and his mother had lived in a town in upstate New York for less than a year. They'd emigrated from India to the US, moving in with Radha's uncle after applying for citizenship. And then, they'd moved to our sleepy little town of Addleton, Pennsylvania. Radha's occupation was listed as seamstress on the form; she worked at a local factory that mostly made curtains.

Why had they moved? Sometimes students and their parents were subject to outer and inner forces that impacted on their lives to such a degree that they felt it necessary to relocate, hoping the change would either solve their problems or somewhat lessen them. A job loss as well as the prospect of a new job opportunity could be a prelude to a move. Unmarried couples who choose to separate as well as divorced couples, both with children, might also conclude that a change of scenery is in order for a variety of reasons. Scandal or tragedy could result in a seeking out a new place to live in an attempt to escape the past and to try to start anew. Or parents might decide to get their kids away from a bad school or neighborhood, with concerns like drug abuse, bullying, or the presence of gangs.

So far, Shivin had been a teacher's dream: he wasn't a behavior problem, and he did all the work that was asked of him. However, the other children didn't want to include him in any group activities. To my great disappointment, even children I had seen exhibit empathy and kindness to others seemed unwilling to interact with him. I had, of course, seen this sort of thing before, a consequence of the harsh reality that children could be cruel and arbitrary in imposing their standards on fellow students. They judged them for acceptable qualities that would most likely include looks, fashion, self-confidence, or a quick wit. Hallmarks, I might add, of those students afforded status for those traits not only by their fellow students, but, sadly, often enough by teachers too.

"He's an unusual boy," I said involuntarily to his mother, realizing immediately afterward how insensitive the remark could seem. "He's very shy, I meant to say."

"It's been that way from birth," she said.

I knew she was referring to his affected eye. It was the first thing I'd noticed about him when he arrived with an admission slip from the office to enroll in my class, and it was no doubt what had created the barrier between him and his classmates.

"Wouldn't an operation correct it?" I asked.

She didn't answer me. Her tics and twitching seemed to suddenly get worse. Other than the perfunctory question she'd asked about his performance in school, she did not at all seem to want to talk about Shivin.

He stood alone near the windows. Darkness descended early now as fall drew closer to winter. He reached out and raised the blind over one of the windows and stood there, staring up at the bone-white moon as it cast an eerie, diffuse glow over the night sky.

Through the open door of my classroom, I watched parents with children in tow shuffle past in the hallway. My best student, Lori Singer, an enthusiastic and likeable girl, stood in the back of the room near an aquarium with her parents. She animatedly informed them of the species of each fish, some of the characteristics of those species, and the pet names she and her fellow students had given them. Another student of mine, Brad Demster, a boy who'd been in some trouble for bullying earlier in the year but who'd become less conspicuous in his approach, was accompanied by his mother. She wore an expression of forbearance while her son deposited crumpled papers filled with doodles and candy wrappers into her hands in a joint effort to straighten out his desk. And yet another of my students, Willem Masters, a quiet, intelligent boy, stood with his mother and father. He nodded almost imperceptibly and apprehensively toward the boy looking out the window, even though his back was toward them. His parents looked at each other, their faces betraying concern. The mother grasped her son's hand tightly, and the three of them left the room in haste without having spoken a word to me.

I dreamt about Shivin later, after having seen the eye in full, and in the dream I was struck by how similar the eye was to the moon he'd gazed at through the window in my classroom, bone-white where both the sclera and colored iris should be.

But the pupil... the effect of that pupil – how can one describe it?

In the dream, his mother appeared and nodded knowingly at me, as if to say, "See? See what I mean?" I wondered what kept her tied to the boy, what she'd suffered and endured over the years, and then, I didn't want to think about it.

"Who is his father?" I heard myself ask his mother in the dream.

Her tremors increased to an alarming degree. She looked at me and opened her mouth, but no sound escaped.

The following week, I found my attention drawn repeatedly to Shivin. He exhibited what I initially thought to be an almost pathological display of shyness, but later theorized was a conditioned, self-protective response. Later still, after the fateful event occurred, I discarded that theory in favor of another theory: the eye operated apart somehow, avoiding any attempts by anyone to discover its true nature.

At those rare times he looked at me, the right eye met mine tentatively, but the left seemed to involuntarily wander askew – hence my layman's diagnosis of his condition of a "lazy eye." I'd thought about broaching the subject before in my first and only meeting with his mother, but her appearance and behavior had been unsettling enough to drive the issue from my mind.

It seemed obvious to me that negative reactions by others to the eye resulted in conditioning the boy to avoid social contact. He never raised his hand in class, and it was obviously painful for him to suffer the attention of others when he was called upon to answer a question. His self-esteem was far lower than any child I'd ever encountered. My anger at his mother mounted, feeling she'd done nothing to remedy the situation, and I resolved to contact her and press the issue of some sort of medical treatment or surgery. In the meantime, I was determined to do what I could to help the boy.

The next day, Shivin exhibited the usual behaviors throughout the day – head hanging low, downcast eyes, avoidance of all social interaction with the other students. As the other children were sprinting out of class for recess, I told the boy to wait. It was not my turn to supervise recess, and I'd decided to give up some of my planning time to help him.

"It's all right, Shivin," I said, pulling a chair over and sitting down next to him at his desk. "You don't need to feel ashamed. Look at me."

He looked away. His arms and legs began moving nervously. The expression on his face was a distorted mask of fear and unhappiness.

I took his face in my hands and lifted his head. His eyes met mine and, recoiling in blind panic after only the most fleeting contact with that eye, I toppled over backwards in the chair, scrambling wildly in a desperate effort to flee even before hitting the floor.

What I am about to say cannot come close to actually describing my confrontation with that eye. No experience in my life had come remotely close to the intensity and shock of my encounter with it. I am aware some may say my fear has distorted this account all out of proportion to the truth. But those who know me know I am a person without a flair for the dramatic; in fact, I think they all would describe me as being staid and sober almost to a fault.

In that flicker of a glimpse of that eye, I saw the whole of myself – my life – and the significance of my life in relation to humanity, and humanity's relationship to the universe. And I saw how hopelessly off the mark we'd been, how wrong and twisted most of our ways and ideas are. What we are was not intended, but what that eye reflected was far worse.

I pulled away in sheer terror, overwhelmed in a way that might only be compared to the experience of standing precariously at the edge of an abyss and looking down to discover no end to its depths, courting the intimate immediacy of death to such a degree to awaken the fear inside one to a maddening pitch. And yet, there was something beyond that even more terrifying. One can understand death: when its time has come, it is the irrevocable end, a commonality that connects all living things. Until then, the body and mind reflexively fight to live whenever the threat of it manifests. But this... *this*...

The pull of that eye was more than formidable; it was as though one had been suddenly thrust into the irresistible force of gravity of a world far too large, drawing everything within range into its weighty influence. And, after such an encounter, one's minutes, hours, and days are forever spent trying to escape the effect of coming into contact with it.

And what is it the mind reacts to with such overwhelming terror?

Words fail to communicate it, because it lies beyond the scope of comprehension, and therefore description as well. But what I can say it that it is wholly alien, and the memory of it haunts me still, catching me unawares with the flash of an image, once again fueling the fire of panic that causes my breath to rage in paroxysmal gasps and my heart to race so wildly that it seems that death itself might be my only release.

Fleeing from the classroom not unlike a frightened child who might have been in my charge, I dashed across the playground, through the sea of bewildered faces of children and staff, and out through the nearest gate, focused only on the goal of getting to my car. My hand trembled uncontrollably as I thrust it into my pocket and fumbled for my keys, finally pulling them out to have them drop to the ground. Cursing and sobbing, I snatched the keys up off the ground, located my key fob on the ring, and pressed the button to unlock the door. I got in, started the car, and floored the gas pedal without regard for speed limits or traffic lights, driving until I slammed on the brakes and the car screeched to a stop in front of the building where my apartment was. Shaking all the while like an old man with raging Parkinson's disease, I locked the doors and windows, turned off my cell phone, crawled into bed, and pulled the covers around me tight as another layer of skin.

When daylight finally filtered in through the bedroom windows, I turned my cell phone on and deleted the numerous phone calls I'd received. Then, I called the school. The secretary answered and quickly connected me with the principal. I informed him I was resigning my position effective immediately for personal reasons I could not discuss and from which I would not waver, and hung up. I neither slept nor left my bed that entire night.

I called my brother David in Arizona and asked if he could put me up for a while. We'd never been particularly close, but our parents were dead almost five years now, he was my only sibling, and I desperately needed a place to stay. My friends would have taken me in, but they all either lived in or near Addleton. The reason I decided to turn to David was simple: he lived the farthest from where it had happened.

After packing the car, I got in, intending to drive through town to access the highway. From there, the Garman would get me to my destination. In a daze from lack of sleep and nervous exhaustion, I drove automatically without thinking, until I became aware I was driving past the elementary school. Out in the schoolyard, the chaos of the early lunch recess ruled.

In the corner of the schoolyard furthest from the school building, I saw him. He stood surrounded by a small group of children who taunted him, the leader being the largest of the children, the desk-cleaning bully who'd been to open house with his mother. His head hung down, and one hand shielded his face. The bully lunged forward and pushed him; he staggered back several steps, almost losing his balance. The other children laughed and yelled, goading the bully on.

Suddenly, he raised his head and looked at them. It was the most extraordinary thing: they were momentarily frozen in time, victims of a modern Medusa; then, reanimated, they frantically stumbled and scurried over each other in blind terror, screaming and scattering as they fled from him.

His head slowly turned toward me. I slammed the gas pedal to the floor, squealing tires, laying a thick coat of rubber on the street and a cloud of black smoke in the air as I sped away.

Upon my arrival at David's house in Phoenix, he regarded me with suspicion. I knew he wanted to ask me what the problem was, but I asked him not to press and told him I would explain in time. I assured him I'd done nothing horrific that I'd been fired for, nor committed a crime from which I fled to avoid prosecution.

We'd become strangers to each other in recent years, yet the familial bond remained strong enough for him to accept my request on my terms. He tentatively danced around me, talking about those safe things people talk about when they sense a person is wrestling with something sufficiently disturbing that was best avoided until they were ready. But at that point in time, I had no idea if I would ever be able to talk to him about it. Even though I had put well over two thousand miles between me and the boy, my mind lurched when the faintest hint of a memory of what I'd run from intruded without warning.

He did enough talking for both of us as he caught me up with much I'd missed of his life over the years. He'd done well for himself; he was a junior partner in a law firm. However, he'd been divorced for over six years. They had no children. In the way of an explanation, he told me that the reason the marriage failed was, as his wife Becky stated, he'd married his career. He told me sometimes he yearned for a wife and children, but he agreed Becky was right: his career would afford him little time to spend with a family. We finished the rest of the meal with small talk, chatting about sports and weather and trite gossip involving his neighbors and coworkers until we ran out of things we could even pretend to be interested in, and then we stopped. I felt a kinship with him that I hadn't felt since we'd lived at home together, before he'd left for college and went out into a world that seemed to swallow him up.

I excused myself after supper and apologized, explaining I was exhausted and needed to go to bed. Although I actually was tired, the distance I put between myself and the boy seemed to help. My fatigue might have been the result of the process of my body beginning to slowly relax some of the nervous energy that afflicted me ever since that last fateful encounter with the boy.

My brother had given me the largest of the guest bedrooms. I changed into pajamas, then took my toiletry kit to the bathroom to brush my teeth before turning in.

I looked at my image in the mirror. Apart from a haggardness about my face and a slope-shouldered sag to my body, I looked pretty much the same as usual. However, as I began to brush my teeth I noticed something – the slightest thing. It was my left eye, barely discernible, really, but – were there white flecks within the border of the iris? I felt a momentary surge of panic, but then an inexplicable wave of blissful calm washed over me.

I crawled into bed. A grin broke out over my face, and for some reason I covered it with my hand. There's nothing wrong with my eye, I told myself, just my mind playing tricks on me.

But I would have my brother check it tomorrow, just to be sure.

Allan Rozinski is a writer of fiction and poetry who currently resides in central Pennsylvania. He has most recently had fiction or poetry published in Twilight Times, Heater magazine and the anthology Puppy Love: 2015. He can be found on Facebook.

WICKED TALES

We at Wicked Tales and DAOwen Publications would like to thank you for purchasing a copy of the Muffled Scream anthology. Without your interest it would not come to be.

Please take the time to rate this book on GoodReads and/or whichever outlet you purchased it. In this way the audience will grow and we can bring to you Muffled Scream II: A Scratch at the Door in 2017.

Again, thank you for purchasing a copy of Muffled Scream.

Douglas Owen
Editor

www.ingramcontent.com/pod-product-compliance
Lightning Source LLC
Chambersburg PA
CBHW061234170626
46809CB00007B/2679